Heaping Spoonful

Shauna Glenn

authorHOUSE®

AuthorHouse™
1663 Liberty Drive, Suite 200
Bloomington, IN 47403
www.authorhouse.com
Phone: 1-800-839-8640

First published by AuthorHouse 7/9/2008

ISBN: 978-1-4343-8453-9 (sc)
ISBN: 978-1-4343-8454-6 (hc)

Library of Congress Control Number: 2008906313

Printed in the United States of America
Bloomington, Indiana

This book is printed on acid-free paper.

for Dadaw

Chapter 1

The pavement pounds beneath my feet. My breath is an extension of me, only free and forceful—visible in the cool morning air. It's barely light outside and there's a slight drizzle. My legs move on auto pilot. I don't even have to think about it—my body just moves. I'm barely present. My clothes, drenched in sweat, cling to me. I run and I run, all the while thinking about how my life has been one huge joke so far. The universe hates me—she's always hated me. Ever since I was that brace-face, freckly, awkward thirteen year old has the universe been my sworn enemy. The day back in middle school during lunch when I got up the nerve to ask Kenny Bower to the Sadie Hawkins dance only to have him spit chocolate milk in my face and then hearing everyone laughing at me as I slumped back over to my table. That's when I first discovered the universe's power over me. I ended up crying myself to sleep that night and begged my mother to let me miss school the next day. She said, "Claire, honey, I know what you're going through must feel like the end of the world, but middle school is supposed to be tortuous—it's

1

everyone's rite of passage. You'll get through it—just hang in there. Besides, I think you're the most beautiful girl in the world and if Kenny what's his name doesn't see that, well, then he's just not worth your time." I think I said something back like, "you have to say that—you're my mom." I remember she smiled and patted me on the head. I didn't understand what she meant, "everyone's rite of passage." At the time, it seemed like she had no clue what she was talking about. She couldn't have understood what I was going through. Parents didn't know what middle school was like.

I eventually got my revenge. The braces came off, I grew taller (and boobs) and set the state's cross country record my sophomore year in high school. I got asked out a lot those days. I was one of the most popular girls. I definitely wasn't the same awkward girl from seventh grade. Kenny Bower even asked me out that year and I politely declined although inside I thought, *there's never chocolate milk around when you need it.*

ଔ ଔ ଔ

As I turned onto Riverdale and headed up the hill, I thought about Bryan—again. He consumes my mind most days and I still can't believe he's gone. It's been 286 days since he died—and it feels like it was yesterday. If I didn't have two children and a business to run, I might have left my life, moved somewhere on the other side of the world, and try and forget him and everything else. But that isn't possible, since someone has to be responsible. Someone has to pick up the pieces of my life that used to be. Someone has to live for both of us.

Tears welled up in my eyes as I remembered my last conversation with Bryan. He was so high on morphine that he was barely conscious most days. But this day, his last day, he was more lucid than he had been in a long time. He called me to his bedside, looked at me and grabbed my hands in his. I started to get upset and he consoled me. *Me.* Here he was, on his death bed, and he was the one telling me everything was going to be OK. He told me he loved me forever and always—and he said he was proud of me. He said I could do this on my own. And he told me I would love again. I shook my head, tears flowing down my cheeks, and I promised him I could never love anybody else. He was my life—he was my love. He smiled once more, squeezed my hands, and then closed his eyes for the last time. A whole hour passed before I let go of his hands.

The last few feet up the hill I was trying my best to push that memory out of my head. I can't do this every day. I can't think about Bryan like this. I know it's not healthy to relive that last moment over and over again. But I'm afraid if I don't, I'll forget him. And I don't want to do that.

I was jolted back to the present when out of nowhere a car came zooming past me and nearly ran me off the road. I screamed "asshole!" and looked around on the ground for something. What? I picked up the biggest rock I could find and hurled it in the direction of the car. It hit the car on the back window and made the loudest smashing sound you've ever heard. Holy shit! I couldn't believe I actually hit the car! I didn't mean to, I was just angry—it was a reflex. I mean how dare a person drive that fast down a residential road? He could've killed me. Then who would raise my children? Huh?

The car came to a screeching halt and the driver must have put the gear in reverse because all of the sudden he came towards me. Oh shit. Oh shit. Oh shit. I turned around and started running the opposite direction. I had to get out of there—and fast. Why was he backing up? Was the guy (I assumed it was a man driving) going to get out and kick my ass? Or kill me?

I ran as fast as I could, but the car caught up to me and the driver threw it in park and jumped out. I noticed then that the license plate said *California* (figures).

"What the fuck is your problem lady?" It was a man and he was pissed! His face was red as a beet and he came storming toward me.

I tried not to act scared but inside I was ready to pee my pants. I crossed my arms across my chest. "My problem? What's your problem? Who do you think you are driving like a maniac down the street?—where children could be playing? You almost ran me down!"

The man looked at the damage to his window and said, "You're paying for this."

I could feel my blood begin to boil. "Oh no I am not! It serves you right for nearly killing me."

"Killing you? Lady, I don't know what your deal is, but I know one thing—you're crazy!"

"Oh yeah? Well, you're, you're—from California. And this is Texas. We don't run down innocent people first thing in the morning. We at least wait until after we've had breakfast."

I didn't know where that came from but it was out of my mouth before I could do anything about it. I had to admit—I did sound a little off my rocker.

The man didn't say anything for a minute. He just stood there, looking at me. I didn't say anything either. I couldn't. It was like all of the sudden time stopped. We were both standing there, frozen—speechless. Someone had to do something. But what? I looked at the cracked window and for a minute felt regret. I started to apologize and offer to pay for it, but before I could get the words out he spouted off, "you know what? Don't worry about this. You got bigger problems than this. I feel sorry for you. No, I take that back. I feel sorry for your *husband*."

It was like a knife to the gut. I wanted to cry. I wanted to scream, *"My husband's dead!"* But I didn't. I fought the tears and I felt the anger well up again in my belly. I looked around for something else to throw at him, but before I could, the man jumped in his car and drove away. I was so mad I couldn't focus. My head was pounding and my heart was racing and I was shaking all over. I don't remember the last few miles back to my house. All I could do was think about what that asshole had said. *He felt sorry for my husband.* Oh yeah? Well who feels sorry for me?

♳ ♳ ♳

When I entered the kitchen door I was still furious. I planned on phoning my dad immediately and telling him what had happened, but seeing my kids sitting at the kitchen table made some of the anger melt away. They smiled up at me and then turned their attention to the Disney channel. It's hard to be mad when you're looking into the faces of the two most perfect children in the world. I decided to be bigger than the asshole with the attitude and focus on the good things—the things right in front of me. I took a deep breath and filled a glass with water. Ana, our nanny/housekeeper was there making breakfast for the kids. She's been with us since my son, Chase, was a baby. He's six now. And my daughter, Allie, is four. They've handled their dad's death pretty well, although I think it's been the hardest on my son. We talk about Bryan every day and Chase is obsessed with his things. I haven't given anything away because my son won't let me. He goes in his dad's closet and touches all his ties and his shirts, and tries to wear his shoes. I stand there sometimes when he doesn't know I'm watching and listen as he talks to Bryan as if he's standing right next to him. He regularly builds a fort in the closet and sleeps some nights curled up in the corner in a pile of Bryan's sweatshirts. The last thing his dad did with him was teach him how to ride a bicycle without training wheels. We talk about that all the time. My daughter has fewer memories of him since she is so young. But I made a poster of all the pictures of her and Bryan and hung it on the wall in her room. We look at it together and she asks me, "what were we doing in this picture?" or she'll say, "That was a funny day with Daddy."

I leaned down and kissed each of my children on the cheek, said "good morning," and then retreated to my room. Just as I was peeling off my clothes to take a shower, the phone rang. *Already?* I picked it up on the third ring and before I could say anything, my sister, Lucy, was already talking a hundred miles an hour.

"You're still coming to dinner at my apartment tonight, right? I mean I've made your favorite—chicken parmesan. The kids like that, right? If not, I've got a frozen pizza."

She was still rambling on. "Lucy. *Lucy!*"

"What?"

"Slow down. I can barely understand you. How much coffee have you had this morning?"

She laughs. "My usual—three cups. Oh Claire, I'm *really* excited for you to meet Drew. I think he might be the *one*. Be here at seven sharp." And then she hung up the phone.

Oy vey. My sister and her many boyfriends. In the last two years, she's had seventeen—that we know of. There was the juggler, the mechanic, the guy who lied about being a tax attorney (why anyone would make that up is beyond me), the school teacher, the ex football player and the sky diving instructor. Those are just the ones I can rattle off the top of my head. I never get real involved with any of these men because they're usually here and gone by the time I learn their names. So why this Drew person would be any different is a mystery. I already felt sorry for the guy.

6

After I got ready for the day, I drove the kids to their schools, dropped off the cleaning and headed downtown. We live in a suburb of Dallas. It used to be rather small, but Dell opened a facility nearby—and boom! The people started pouring in. In the last three years, our small community has gone from ten thousand people to about a hundred thousand (I could be exaggerating a little, but I know it's a huge number). There are new schools, more restaurants, a mega-mall and housing developments going in everywhere. But downtown has remained virtually the same. There's a town square with quaint little boutiques, antique stores, a diner, art galleries, and my store—Heaping Spoonful. It's a bakery that I opened seven years ago, right after Bryan and I got married.

He was a bonds trader with Merrill Lynch and worked eighty hour weeks. I didn't know what I wanted to do with my life, but had always liked to cook and enjoyed being around people. My degree was art history which is practically useless unless you want to be a school teacher or a docent at the museum. Neither one of those things appealed to me, so I opted for plan C. Bryan and I took out a loan and I rented what I deemed the space. Soon after that, I went to work painting, laying tile, buying furniture, ovens, counter stands and refrigerators. Bryan was too busy to help so I relied a lot on my mom and dad. They live only a few miles from downtown, so it was convenient for them. My dad was also retired from being a school principal—which made it convenient for me. Since then, Heaping Spoonful has been a prosperous little business. I have some really good regular customers and the booming growth in the population has helped, too. My sister Lucy works with me and my dad does, too—when he's not with my mother.

My mother was diagnosed with Alzheimer's three years ago at the age of sixty-seven. Last year, right before Bryan died, my dad decided to put her in a nursing home. He couldn't take care of her by himself anymore. She was getting up during the night and leaving the house. Once, their neighbor, Mr. Tomlinson, called at three in the morning to let my dad know my mother was sitting in his living room, telling stories about when she was a little girl. Apparently she rang their doorbell and when they opened the door to see who it was, my mother was standing there, wearing nothing but a short, thin nightgown and a pair of my dad's tube socks pulled up to her knees. It was thirty degrees outside. That was when my dad knew he couldn't care for her. He was sixty-nine himself. He's always felt guilty for putting her in a nursing home, but he really had no other choice. Lucy and I let him know we totally supported and agreed with his decision.

I pulled into the back lot of the bakery and parked my car by the door. I entered the store and found Maria, Ben and Celia in the kitchen. Lucy would normally be here but asked for the day off so she could clean her apartment for her new boyfriend, Drew. The thought of the whole thing made me roll my eyes. I'm not sure my sister will ever grow up. She's thirty-three and acts twelve.

"Good morning," I said to them as I put on my apron. "How's everything going so far today?"

Celia turned to me and said, "We're out of the chocolate-chip walnut scones and banana bread."

I looked to my kitchen manager, Ben. "OK then, we'll have to fix that."

Ben saluted and said, "Yes, ma'am."

Maria handed me a message. It was from the food supplier. It said *no more strawberries.*

She furrowed her brow and asked, "How are we going to sell chocolate covered strawberries if we have no strawberries?"

"I'll call around and see what I can do," I said. That seemed to appease her because she softened and went back to removing peanut butter bars from the cookie sheet.

Just then the bell rang, indicating someone had come in the front door. I waved, "I'll do this," and headed to the front. It was Mrs. Sugarman, one of the customers that helps keep this place open. She buys more bread, dinner rolls, cakes and cookies than one person could possibly eat, especially someone as teeny as her. She's eighty-five years old and weighs about that much, too. She has more money than anyone else within a fifty-mile radius. Her family owned most of the land in this part of town and everyone knows who they are. She's the oldest living Sugarman left and she couldn't be sweeter if she tried. Every time I see her she's dressed in couture and always has on some sort of fur coat. It doesn't matter if it's August and a hundred degrees outside, she wears fur.

Today she's wearing a black pantsuit, with a leopard print coat and a black pillbox hat. Her lipstick is shockingly red and her shoes are of the old lady kind. Melvin, her driver, stands by the front door just like he does every other day.

I greet her and we exchange smiles.

"What can I help you with today, Mrs. Sugarman?"

"Well, you know those oatmeal raisin cookies I bought the other day?"

"Yes, ma'am."

"I need two dozen more, and a loaf of monkey bread."

"You got it." I looked toward Melvin and asked, "Coffee?"

Melvin removed his hat and came toward the counter. I poured him a cup of his favorite, the dark roast with chicory. I dropped in two sugar cubes and handed him the cup and a spoon. "Thank you, Ms. Claire," he said as he went back to standing by the front door.

I finished Mrs. Sugarman's order while she nibbled on the samples I had sitting out. I walked around the counter and stood in front of her. Melvin came and took the boxes from me and Mrs. Sugarman asked, "Claire, how's your mama?"

"She's doing all right. I haven't been to see her in a couple of days."

"Well then you better get up there and see her." And she turned to leave.

"Yes, ma'am, I will."

Mrs. Sugarman stopped and turned back around to face me. "Have you ever met my grandson, Henry?"

"No, ma'am, I don't believe I have."

She smiled at me. "You ought to meet him. He's a nice young man."

"OK, maybe I will someday. See you next time."

Melvin opened the door for Mrs. Sugarman and I stood at the window and watched as he helped her get to the car. I stood there realizing what a fragile little person she really was. Then I thought about what Mrs. Sugarman had said about meeting her grandson. The very idea sickened me. I mean, really, it was ridiculous. I wasn't ready. I'm *not* ready. Besides, I imagine he's twenty-something and spoiled rotten. That's the last thing I needed or wanted to be involved in, but he sounded perfect for Lucy. Mrs. Sugarman had been right about one thing though—I needed to see my mom.

Ↄ Ↄ Ↄ

After putting in a full day at the bakery, I made my way back toward the house. The kids would be home by now. Chase is in the first grade and Allie's in preschool. Ana picks her up after lunch and takes her home for a nap. Then the two of them drive to Chase's elementary school at three. When I get home, Ana leaves and it's just the three of us until the next morning.

When Bryan and I decided to have children, we planned on sending them to private school. But when he got sick, we knew without his large income we wouldn't be able to do it. The bakery does all right, but not enough to pay for private school. Bryan worked so hard so that we could have everything for our family. Sometimes I feel like that's what killed him—his working hard to give us everything. He started getting tired a lot. He would come home from work around seven and fall asleep before eating dinner. On the weekends he would sleep in until ten or eleven, but neither of us thought anything about it. When he lost his appetite and then twenty pounds, it alarmed me. His eyes weren't clear anymore and his face was always flushed. Then he started having night sweats and running a fever. He kept saying he must have the flu, but he never got better. And he kept killing himself at work. Finally, after months of my riding him, he went to the doctor. Test after test was performed and that's when we got the diagnosis—stage IV Hodgkin's Lymphoma. And there was nothing we could do. It was too late, the doctors said. The cancer had spread into his vital organs and we were told he had very little time—maybe a few months if he was lucky. I wanted to die. I was so angry with him for not going to the doctor sooner. How could he do this to me—to our family? We were sitting in the office of the oncologist and I begged the doctor, "Tell me. If we had found out a few months ago, would we have been able to treat it?"

The doctor, sitting behind his desk, looked from me to Bryan and nodded his head. "Most likely. The odds are in your favor then."

I broke down in his office and turned to face Bryan. I started screaming, "Why didn't you go to the doctor when I told you to? You're going to die and there's nothing I can do now. This is your fault!" I got up from my chair and began hitting Bryan in the chest. He grabbed me, wrapped his arms around me and broke down. We stood in the office, both of us crying, for nearly an hour. At some point, the doctor left the room. When we finally pulled ourselves together, we tried to figure out what to do for the time he had left. And we had to figure out a way to tell the children their daddy was going to die. When I thought about them, I started to cry again. They would never really know this man. They were going to grow up without a dad—and knowing that nearly killed me.

Chapter 2

We arrived at Lucy's apartment at seven o'clock sharp—just as we'd been instructed. We knocked on the door and entered, all of us yelling, "Hello! We're here."

The music was thumping. It was so loud that my teeth began to chatter. The kids put their hands over their ears and as I made my way to the stereo to turn it down, I wondered where my idiot sister could be. Chase turned on the Xbox and started playing a video game (See? I told you my sister is twelve!) and Allie tugged at my leg saying, "hold me." I picked her up and together we walked toward the bedroom. Just then my dad came in and I turned to him and waved. He asked, "Where's Lucy?" Before I could say, "I'm wondering the same thing," I pushed the door open to her room and found Lucy, naked, pinned up against the wall by a very naked man (all I could see was his backside) and they were having what appeared to be—sex. Lucy saw me and screamed.

I gasped, covered Allie's eyes and ran into the other room where my dad was standing. I started laughing and my dad asked, "What is it?"

Allie squealed, "I saw a man's bobo."

Dad asked, "What?"

"Nothing. Never mind. Lucy will be out in a minute." I hoped this wasn't what she was serving for an appetizer.

I went in the kitchen to find the wine. We must have wine now. My dad followed me into the kitchen, helped me find the bottle opener and uncorked a nice bottle of Pinot Grigio. We sipped our wine in silence. OK, well I didn't exactly sip mine—it was more like gulping. But I couldn't help it. I couldn't get the image out of my mind—of my sister, fucking some strange guy up against the wall, just minutes before she was expecting company. The more I thought about it, the more pissed off I got. I mean, I've got small kids over here for Christ's sake. But rather than say something right now, I decided to wait until tomorrow. There was no need in ruining her dinner. I looked around. It appeared she had gone to a lot of trouble. The apartment was spotless. She had set the table with real dishes and real glasses and real silverware. The chicken parmesan smelled delicious and she had even made a salad and some sort of dessert concoction.

As I was downing the rest of my first glass of many o'glasses of wine that night, Lucy and the man I assumed was her new beau, entered the kitchen. Lucy looked disheveled and embarrassed and by the look on my dad's face, he now knew what had been going on. He simply shook his head and poured another glass of wine—for the both of us. Lucy turned to me as if to say "sorry" and then went on to introduce Drew. He had his back to us at first—apparently enraptured with the car racing game that Chase was playing. When Lucy got his attention he turned to face us and at that moment I thought I was going to vomit right then and there.

It was him. It was the arrogant, asshole, California license plate guy from this morning. The same guy who nearly ran me down is having sex with my sister. No wonder he liked watching Chase play the race car game. It was good practice for *actual* car racing—something he knew a lot about. All of the sudden I couldn't breathe. It felt as if a ton of weight was crushing my chest. I was still holding Allie at this point, but was afraid that my arms might give and she would fall to the floor. I rearranged my grip on her and held her a little tighter to me. I held my breath, waiting to see if he recognized me. He smiled as he shook hands with my dad and then as he reached for mine (which, by the way wasn't extended), stopped short.

"Have we met somewhere before?"

I wasn't sure if words would be able to form, but then managed, "if you mean, did you nearly run over me this morning, then yes."

The color disappeared from his face and then he covered his mouth with his hand. I felt heat washing over my entire body and my heart started pounding.

Lucy asked, "What's going on? Claire, what are you talking about?"

Drew pointed at me and said to Lucy, "this is her. This is the crazy woman who cracked my back window this morning."

Lucy's mouth fell open—as she was obviously shocked by this news—and my dad seemed very confused. I put Allie down and told her to go play with Chase. She ran off and immediately Chase yelled, "Mom, tell Allie she's too little to play this game!"

I ignored them and turned my attention to Drew. I hadn't noticed earlier that he was so good looking. He was your typical California surfer boy. His hair was sun bleached and his skin tanned. He had a great body (I'd already been privy to naked Drew thanks to the peep show minutes earlier) and his piercing green eyes sent a shiver up my spine.

What was I thinking? I had to focus. This asshole was no one to be admired. He was a jerk with a lead foot and a nasty temper. So what if he was smoking hot. We don't like him, remember?

And I was about to tell him exactly that when Lucy said, "Wait a minute. Claire, that was you? You threw a rock at his car?"

"Yes, but he started it." Wow. Who was twelve now?

We all began talking and yelling at once. No one could get a word in. I was yelling at Drew, Drew was yelling at me, Lucy was yelling at the both of us.

My dad got in the middle of the huddle and screamed, "Wait a minute, *wait a minute*! Everyone stop yelling! I want to know what's going on—and I want one person at a time to tell me."

I raised my hand as if I were in middle school all over again. "Yes, Claire," my dad said.

Drew raised his hand and pointed to the wine. "Do you mind? I'm going to need some of that."

It almost made me laugh. I said *almost*.

After Drew poured the wine, I recounted my side of the story and every time Drew went to interrupt me, the principal in my dad would say, "Just a minute, Drew. You'll get your turn."

The whole thing was completely ridiculous. I told what really happened, and then Drew lied and made up a completely preposterous story. What a liar he was turning out to be.

In the end my dad asked me, "Did you throw a rock and crack his window?"

"Yes, Daddy, but…"

"No, no, Claire. No buts. It's a simple yes or no answer."

"Yes," I said as I stared daggers at Drew's head.

"Then you have to pay for it."

I looked at my dad. "What? I'm not paying for it! You can forget it!"

My dad shook his head at me and said, "It's the right thing to do and you know it. I raised you better than that."

16

He might as well have kicked me in the stomach. Why do parents have to play that card? Here I am, almost forty years old and my dad can still make me feel like a little kid.

"Fine. I'll pay for it, but I'm not happy about it."

"Noted," my dad said.

Lucy let out a huge sigh and said, "Can we eat now? I'm starving."

My dad looked at her with disapproving eyes and said, "Not so fast, Lucy Goosey. Let's chat in your room for a minute."

Dad and Lucy left the room for what I expected would be the birds and the bees talk. My dad—bless his heart. I swear he still thinks of us as little girls with freckles and pig-tails.

While they were gone, Drew opened another bottle of wine and offered me some. I let him pour it and even mustered a "thank you."

He started to make conversation and say something about the kids when I turned to him, cut him off and said, "Look, I'll write you a check, but don't talk to me. Don't take my giving in as a sign of weakness. I'm doing this for my sister who apparently likes you for God knows what reason. And that's all. So don't try and chit chat with me—or tell me how great my kids are—or say anything else that might pop into that overly bleached head of yours. We're not friends. Besides, you won't be in the picture long. They never are."

We made it through dinner although you could cut the tension with a knife. No one spoke. The only audible sound was the clanging of the silverware against the plates. Lucy was upset, I could tell. It obviously wasn't going exactly how she'd planned. Part of that was my fault. The older sister in me felt bad for her. After dinner, we took our dessert (Side note: turns out it was chocolate pudding with crumbled up Oreo cookies and gummy worms—made to look like dirt and worms—I decided to pass—the girl works in a bakery for Christ's sake—she couldn't have brought home a lemon chess pie or a red velvet cake?) and moved to the living room. Dad tried to lighten the mood by asking how the two of them met—like he really cared. But this seemed to excite Lucy. She yelled, "let me tell it, let me tell it." Drew smiled at her and said, "The floor's all yours."

Anyone got a barf bag? I think I'm going to be sick.

Lucy proceeded to tell us about how she and Drew met at the Hard Rock Hotel and Casino in Las Vegas a year ago. They really hit it off, but when she left the hotel, forgot to get his number and he lost hers, yada, yada, yada. Then, a few weeks ago, Drew found the number in a jacket pocket and called her out of the blue. The two of them have been talking on the phone ever since and then he decided to come out and stay with her for awhile.

That's when my dad asked, "What do you do, Drew?"

"Oh, I'm a musician. I play the bass guitar."

This got Chase's attention. "Cool. Can you teach me how to play?"

Before I could say, "No, he cannot," Drew said, "Sure little man—anytime."

My dad continued the inquisition. "Do you have a regular job playing the guitar or is this something you do on the side—say after you get off work from your *real* job?"

Lucy cut Dad a look and I snorted a laugh. Good one, Fred. That's my dad's name—Fred. My mom's name is Ethel. Not really. It's Mary. But it would be awesome if it was Ethel—*or Wilma?*

Anyway, Drew said to my dad, "I play in a band called The Cafeteria Ladies. You may have heard of us."

My dad shook his head and said, "No, I'm not up on the music scene since the Beach Boys broke up."

Lucy jumped up. "Oh, you've *got* to listen to them. They're awesome. I was playing it on the CD player awhile ago."

I got up to refill my wine for the sixth or seventh time (who's counting?) and said, "We heard it when we came in. It was awful—and then I saw my sister's face (so I changed it to)—awful-ly different."

Lucy turned it on again and for the next fifteen minutes we sat there listening to titles such as *"Slash Her Face Out of My Mind," "The Devil's Cooking Up Something Good This Time,"* and my personal favorite, *"Kill Whitey."*

My dad looked scared for his little girl and my kids were jumping up and down with their hands over their ears. Someone in the apartment below us started banging on the ceiling and that was my cue that it was time to leave. I cleared the rest of the plates, rinsed them off and put them in the dishwasher. There appeared to be no soap to put *in* the dishwasher, but instead of offering to run to the store for her (what I would normally do in this situation) I decided to let her figure this out for herself—for once. I was a bit woozy from all the wine so my dad offered to drive us home. I spoke briefly in Drew's direction—telling him to let me know when he had an estimate for the window, and then I kissed my sister goodbye.

The last thing I said to her before leaving was, "Don't be late to work tomorrow."

She rolled her eyes at me as she shut the door. Was I glad *that* was over!

On the way home my kids fell asleep in the car. It was a quiet drive and after a few minutes my dad asked, "Do you think Lucy will ever grow up?"

"I have no idea. Why? Do you worry about her?"

My dad smiled at me and said, "I worry about both my girls. But for different reasons."

"Why do you worry about me?" I asked.

"Because you are obviously angry with the world. You seem to think the universe has some longstanding vendetta against you and it simply isn't true. What's happening to you is life. You get some bad and you get some good. But it seems to me you fail to see the good. You only see the bad things that have happened. And that makes me sad for you. So I worry. I worry you won't let yourself be happy. I worry you won't find the good anymore. Just look in the backseat. That's good."

I turned around and stared at the faces of my sleeping children. I felt hot tears well up in my eyes. My dad was right about me. I am mad at the world.

"You know, it takes a lot of energy to be sad and feel sorry for yourself all the time. Why don't you cut yourself a break and let it go for awhile. Try and have some fun."

"OK, Daddy, I'll try," I lied.

Chapter 3

On my way to the bakery the next day, I went by the nursing home to visit my mother. She was in her usual spot in her room, sitting in a chair, facing the window. She looked nice. She was wearing a sundress and her hair was pulled up in a neat bun. This must be a good day. Sometimes the aides try to dress her and she revolts and starts calling them names. Other days she refuses to get out of bed—she screams that they're hurting her. All of this was a little too much to take in at first. We had never known someone with Alzheimer's before my mother and we had no idea how much she would change—how she would become someone we didn't recognize. This was a slow death. And it was so hard for my dad. He tried his best every day to be strong, to keep going, to make sure everyone else was OK. In a way my tragedy had been easier. When we found out that Bryan was going to die from cancer it was like OK, this is going to happen soon. But with someone with Alzheimer's, you live every day like you just found out you were sick. Some days are good—she remembers who we are. Others are not so good—we're strangers who just sort of look alike.

I kneeled in front of her and said hello. She looked at me, smiled and asked, "Have you seen the box with the pink bow?"

I stood up, pulled a chair next to her and asked, "What box with the pink bow?"

She straightened up in her chair and said a little more sternly, "the box with the pink bow. You need to find the box with the pink bow."

I had no idea what she was talking about but she seemed to be getting upset by this. "All right, mother. I'll find it. Where is it?"

"You need the box with the pink bow."

"OK," I said. "I'll find it."

I looked all over her room but found no box. I looked under the bed and in the closet. When one of the aides came in I asked her about a box with a pink bow. She said she hadn't seen such a box.

I went back to sitting next to my mother and held her hand in mine. "You look pretty today, Mama."

"Thank you, Claire."

When she said my name it took me by surprise. Outside of repeating that I needed to find the box with the pink bow, she had spent the rest of the time staring out the window and I wasn't sure she even knew I was there anymore. I patted her hand and put it back in her lap. I leaned in to kiss her cheek and she turned to face me. She hadn't done that in so long. Most days she didn't look at any of us in the face.

"Don't stop looking for the box with the pink bow."

CҘ   CҘ   CҘ

When I got to the bakery, Lucy was loading up the van for a delivery. She met me at the door and said, "I wish you hadn't been such a jerk to Drew. I really like him, you know."

I was taken aback. I wasn't expecting this from Lucy. I immediately got defensive.

I crossed my arms, raised my voice and said, "Well I wasn't expecting to walk in on you having sex your latest boy-toy. Oh yeah, and I had my children with me! Allie saw the both of you naked, and humping! How exactly are you going to explain to a four year old what you were doing?"

"Well, I am sorry for that. Is she OK?"

"Yes, she's fine." And then I softened. "She probably doesn't even remember. I, on the other hand, am scarred for life." We both started to laugh. I couldn't help but picture them in my mind again. I especially remembered Drew's bare ass.

Then I got serious again. "But what is it with you and that man?"

"Drew. His name is Drew. And why do you care? What's your problem with him? That he's too perfect?"

Is she crazy? "I was going to say too flawed."

"Look, Claire. I'm sorry Bryan died. I wish he hadn't. But you can't expect everyone else around you to stop living just because you have."

I felt as if she punched me in the stomach. "I haven't stopped living— I'm just trying to find a new way to do it. I don't think I've been very successful so far."

"Well that's the understatement of the universe."

I couldn't help but laugh. What she said about me was true.

"Are we OK?" I asked.

"Of course," Lucy said as she gave me a hug.

I pulled away from her and said, "I still don't like what's his name."

ি ি ি

Mrs. Sugarman came in this morning and bought nearly everything out of the case. She was having a garden party at her house and needed lots of baked goodies. I was short-handed because Maria was out sick, Ben had the day off and Lucy was out on delivery. That left Celia and I to man the store by ourselves. I went to the kitchen to get more blueberry muffins and when I returned, found an unwanted visitor standing at the counter. Drew was there, making small talk with Mrs. Sugarman, who had obviously been sizing him up. He *was* a little out of place, wearing his Green Peace t-shirt, khaki pants and flip flops. His aviator sunglasses were holding back the bangs on top of his head and for the first time, I really noticed his eyes. They were the color of emeralds. I'd never seen eyes so green. He wasn't exactly the picture of someone you'd guess played guitar in a heavy metal band. He looked more like an Abercrombie & Fitch model. But that was beside the point. He was a fungus and I didn't like him. Why did I have to keep reminding myself that point?

I tried ignoring him, but I could feel his eyes on me so I turned to him and asked, "What is it that you want? Don't you have somewhere else you need to be?—someone else to run down?—more children to corrupt with your devil music?"

Drew sighed and looked down at the floor. I wondered what he was thinking—sort of. But before he had the chance to say anything I added, "Do you have an estimate for me? You didn't have to come all the way down here. You could've given it to Lucy."

Mrs. Sugarman leaned in a little closer. "Claire, dear?"

"Just a minute Mrs. Sugarman," I said in her direction before turning my attention back to Drew. "I mean, what *are* you doing here? Lucy's out. And you shouldn't come by here while she's working."

Drew laughed. "I didn't come here to see Lucy. I came here to make amends with you. I think we got off on the wrong foot."

Mrs. Sugarman again said, "Excuse me, Claire?"

"Hold on one second, Mrs. Sugarman," I said without looking her way. By now I was stuffing croissants in a bag—and not delicately either. "You're wasting your time. I'm done. Let's just agree that we don't like each other and get on with our lives. I will be civil to you for the sake of Lucy, OK?" I tossed a croissant his way. "See, I'm even sharing my food with you."

At this point I had got a box and was filling it with cookies—lots of cookies. I wasn't even sure who it was for.

"If I could just..." Mrs. Sugarman started to say and then, "JUST A MINUTE, MRS. SUGARMAN!" Drew and I shouted at her at the same time.

Drew and I looked at each other and laughed. I quickly turned to Mrs. Sugarman, who seemed stunned by our outburst. I went to the other side of the counter, helped her to a table, and yelled at Celia to take over helping her while I dealt with California boy. I grabbed Drew by the hand and pulled him to the kitchen. Once inside I had no idea what I was going to say to him. We stood there for a minute, neither of us saying anything. We were just starring at each other. And his eyes sort of had me entranced. He was eerily beautiful. And the weird thing was—it wasn't an uncomfortable silence. It was good. I couldn't even remember why I'd been so angry with him. It was like I'd fallen under some voodoo spell. I don't know what came over me, but all of the sudden I reached up, grabbed his face and pulled it to mine. I kissed him hard on the mouth. It felt like it lasted forever and it was good—no, it was fucking great. I hadn't felt so alive in a long time. I hadn't kissed another man in almost ten years. He kissed me deeper and when he did, I felt a familiar tingle. I was sure I was melting or floating—something. But I was sure my legs would no longer hold me up.

He pulled away first and I was quickly jolted back to the present. I thought of my sister. Lucy! Oh my God, what had I just done? My face must have said it all because Drew pushed the hair out of my eyes and said, "I'm sorry for doing that—OK, that's not true—I'm not sorry at all." He smiled at me and I instantly knew what Lucy had seen in him after all.

"You didn't do it. I did. And now I know for sure that I'm the worst sister on the planet."

Drew leaned in closer and whispered in my ear, "Do you want to do it again?"

 C3   C3   C3

I woke up from a dream I was having. I was swimming naked in the ocean and the waves crashed over my head again and again. I felt a hand on my stomach and then I realized it wasn't a dream at all. It was Drew's hand that was on me. And I suddenly remembered where I was. After throwing my better judgment and any moral code I once possessed out the window, I left with Drew and we rented a hotel room. It only took a second to undress and completely get lost in each other's bodies. It wasn't long before I remembered what I'd been missing this last year. And I knew one thing for sure—I didn't want to wait this long ever again. People who say they don't enjoy sex aren't doing it right. And he was amazing.

After rolling around on the bed for several hours, we had both fallen asleep. Reality was now setting in. I sat up, careful not to wake him, and checked the time. It was three o'clock. I'd been gone almost the whole day. I grabbed my cell phone—fifteen missed calls—most of them from Lucy. Shit! Did she know?

I jumped out of the bed and started pulling my clothes on. Drew woke up and lay there, watching me. I saw his smile and couldn't help but want to eat every inch of him. I fought the urge and said, "Get up. Get dressed. We have to go. I've got to get home to my kids."

Just then I heard his cell phone vibrate. He picked it up off the table and read the number. "It's Lucy, isn't it?" I asked. I was sure I was going to hell now.

"Yep. She's called a lot."

"Shit, shit, shit, shit. What do we do?"

Drew got up and started dressing at a snail's pace. It wasn't fast enough for me so I went to him and attempted to help him dress faster. We tripped over each other and he fell to the bed. "You know, this will go a lot faster if you let me do it myself."

"Sorry. Can you please hurry? And you didn't answer my question about Lucy. What do we do?"

"There's nothing to do. You detest me. I loathe you. So we had sex to see who hated who more." Drew finished putting on his flip flops and grabbed his sunglasses from the night stand. "Are you making a joke? Because this is no time for jokes. This is my little sister—and she really likes you."

"Lucy's a big girl. Besides you weren't too worried about your little sister an hour ago."

He was right. I did this. I wanted this. Oh, did I want this. Now the only thing left to do was tell her, move, or pretend it never happened. I think I'll go with number three.

Chapter 4

I couldn't sleep. I kept thinking about Lucy, and Drew, and how I'd totally messed up this time. What kind of a person am I anyway? I've always thought of myself as one that is decent, with high moral standards, but yesterday I proved otherwise. It's just that I couldn't help it. It was like this ravenous beast was inside of me and I couldn't keep it caged any longer—nor did I want to. But now it's so much for the afterglow. I feel guilty. No, guilty would imply that I am sorry. I'm not sorry. Well, I am sorry but not for the reasons you would think. I'm sorry for Lucy—that I betrayed her. And from this moment on I will do my best to prove that I am a sister worth keeping. But I'm not sorry that it happened.

Since sleep was apparently out of the question, I got up around four and washed three loads of laundry, baked banana nut bread and tried not to think about Drew. There was absolutely no reason to give him any more thought because this was not going any further. We kissed, we shagged, we said goodbye—end of story. And if my sister had any sense, she would do the same thing (which, if history continues to repeat itself, the whole thing will be over in the next few days anyway).

Around six, Ana arrived and I took off for my morning run. Surely I would be able to clear my head. My thoughts went from Drew and Lucy to something my mother kept saying when I visited her last. She mentioned a box with a pink bow. I had no idea what that meant, but she was so persistent. With her illness though, you never know if what she's saying involves something from the present or from when she was a little girl. For all I know, the box with a pink bow could be something she had when she was seven.

After dropping the kids off at school, I decided to take my time getting to the bakery. I wasn't sure how I would act around Lucy. Would I give myself away? I hoped not. And I hadn't even considered the thought that Drew might have told her. Surely he's not that stupid. But he *is* a man—so really all bets are off.

I turned left onto Magnolia Terrace and parked in front of my parents' house. I ran up to the door and knocked twice on it before opening it and yelling out, "Daddy! It's Claire!"

I went over and poured myself some coffee. I popped two slices of bread into the toaster and was waiting for it to brown when my dad appeared and said, "I wasn't expecting you, but it's nice to see you."

He came toward me and kissed me on the cheek. I smiled at him and said, "I wanted to come by and ask you about something that Mother kept mentioning the other day." I sat down at the kitchen table and buttered my toast. Then I slathered on a thick layer of apricot preserves.

My dad joined me at the table and asked, "Oh? What's that?"

I took a bite and tried my best to talk with my mouth full. "She kept saying something about a box with a pink bow. Do you know anything about it?"

He seemed to be thinking. "It doesn't ring a bell. What did she say about it?"

"Nothing, really. She just kept saying it over and over again. She was very persistent."

My dad reached over and snagged the last piece of toast. "I know, Claire. But it could mean nothing. She rattles on about stuff all the time. The other day she kept saying 'chocolate pudding' so I had the aide bring her some. She ended up throwing it against the wall."

The image of that made me laugh. My mother never would have done something like that in the past. She is a southern woman and polite to boot. You could stomp on her foot with your high-heeled, steel-toed boot and she would say, "Excuse me, please. Would you mind terribly removing your boot from the top of my foot?—If you don't mind, of course." So she would absolutely die if she knew she behaved in such a way.

I thought for a minute and then asked, "Do you mind if I take a look in the attic? Maybe it's up there. Maybe it's something she wants."

"Be my guest," he said. He got up and started to walk out of the room. Then he turned and said, "Feel free to organize the mess while you're up there."

"No, thank you," I said. "I've seen it and we're better off having a bonfire."

"That's your mother. She keeps everything."

God, was he right about the attic. There was so much shit piled everywhere, I had to be careful where I stepped. He was also right about the amount of stuff that my mother had accumulated over the years—boxes of clothes, pictures and artwork that Lucy and I made in elementary school, our old cheerleading uniforms and *Southern Living* magazines—everywhere. Why she would want half of this shit was beyond me. I rifled through box after box, but found nothing with a pink bow. As I was making my way back to the stairs, I saw something out of the corner of my eye. There, sitting on an old parsons chair, was a big white box with a pink bow. I almost didn't see it because it was covered in at least four inches of dust. I was careful not to step on the wrong place and subsequently fall through the ceiling. I finally reached the place where the box was sitting. It was dark and I couldn't see very well, plus the fact that it was kind of spooky up there, so I lifted the box and carefully carried it down the stairs and to the kitchen. Before opening it, I wet a paper towel and cleaned off the top of it. There was no sense in making a mess. As I lifted the lid, I was astounded by what I found inside. Recipes. Lots and lots of recipes. They were so old that the paper was brittle thin and worn, and the ink faded. You could barely read them. Some of them were dated back to the 1890's. They were my grandmother's mother's recipes. And my mother wanted me to have them. I felt like I'd hit the jackpot.

CB CB CB

When I entered her room, my mother was painting her fingernails. I couldn't believe it! I hadn't seen her do anything for herself in a long time. It made me so happy. She looked up at me and smiled. "Well, hello Claire. How are the children? You've got to bring them to see me soon."

I was shocked. "Mama, you know who I am? You remember Chase and Allie?"

"Honey, I may be old, but I'm not crazy."

"Of course you're not, Mother. I just meant..."

"I know what you meant. Now, tell me everything."

I didn't know where to start. My mother hadn't been present like this since before we put her here. It was like she came out of her Alzheimer's coma and was completely her old self again. I pulled up a chair next to her and then I thought about my dad. I should call him. He should see her like this.

I looked in her eyes. They were twinkling and bright and absolutely beautiful. "Just a minute, Mama. I want to call Daddy and tell him you're having a good day."

She dismissed me saying, "Don't call. He'll be here soon enough. I want to talk to you. I want to know how *you* are. Did you find the box with the pink bow?"

My eyes lit up. "Yes. That's why I came by—to thank you. I had no idea you had all of your great grandmother's recipes. They're wonderful."

"I knew you'd appreciate them. I know you'll figure out what to do with them." My mother beamed. She seemed so proud of herself.

I tried to smile again but something came over me and I started to cry. I covered my face with my hands and sobbed. My mother put her arms around me and tried to soothe me. It was incredible. I had my mom back. It was what I'd wanted and now she was really here. She was really listening. I stopped crying, took a deep breath, and told her everything. I told her about how angry I'd been at everyone; I told her about Drew and how I'd done a horrible thing to Lucy. I told her about Chase's obsession with Bryan's clothes and how he seemed to be fighting to hang on to his dad's memory. I told her I was sad for Allie and I told her I felt sad for myself.

She placed her hand under my chin and said to me, very sternly, "Listen here, Claire. You need to grow up and stop all this nonsense. You are a very capable woman and I know you can do this. You have to do this. You have to be strong for those children—teach them about the world and about loss and about love. Now you stop being sad for yourself and live the best life you know how."

I wiped my eyes on my sleeve and nodded my head. My mother smiled and kissed me on the forehead. Just then my dad walked in and looked at the two of us. I must have looked a mess. "What's going on in here?"

My mother turned to him and her face lit up. "Fred, I'm so glad to see you."

He looked from her to me and I nodded and said, "She's here."

My dad went to her and they embraced and the two of them talked in a whisper to each other. They looked so happy together. My dad kissed her all over her face and she giggled like a teenage girl. They reminded me of honeymooners. All of the sudden I felt like an intruder. I grabbed my purse and moved towards the door. My mother noticed me leaving and said, "Oh, Claire. Do me a favor and close the door on your way out."

Chapter 5

I knew what I needed to do. I called the bakery. Ben answered and I told them that I would be out for a few days. He asked if everything was OK and I assured him that it was—I just needed some time to myself. He seemed to understand and let me know he had everything under control. We hung up the phone and I called Lucy. Voicemail. I left her a message. I told her that I was going out of town and would be back on Sunday. It was just cryptic enough that I knew as soon as she heard it, she would call me back. I phoned my parents' house and left a message on the answering machine. My dad would still be at the home visiting my mother so I didn't want to call his cell phone and disturb them. Then I went to the kids' schools and took them out early and informed their teachers that they wouldn't be back until Monday.

When the three of us were in the car, Chase asked, "Why'd you come during recess? Am I in trouble?"

I looked at him through the rearview mirror. "No silly. What would you be in trouble for?"

Chase shrugged. "I don't know. But Lance in my class. His dad came to get him from school early one day and he was in big trouble."

"Honey, Lance pulled his pants down and peed in the classroom. That's a big no-no."

Chase started to laugh. "That was funny."

Allie asked, "Where are we going, Mommy?"

I made my voice sound like a cartoon character saying, "On an adventure, my pretty."

They both laughed and yelled in unison, "Do that again."

Then Allie giggled and said, "Say something else in that voice."

And so I did.

We got home and all I told the children was that we were packing our bags and getting on an airplane. I wouldn't tell them where we were going. They whooped and hollered and ran to their rooms. I needed to get in there quickly and help them pack, but first I needed to make a phone call to the bank. After getting the banker on the line, I told him I needed money transferred from my savings account to my checking account. He asked how much. I told him and then he made some comment about how that was a lot of money to be spending so quickly. I wanted to say, "Screw you buddy, why don't you mind your own business?" But I didn't. I was in too good a mood. Instead I said, "sure is, isn't it?" He didn't say anything else. The only sound I heard was the clacking of the computer keys. A few minutes later the transaction was completed and we were one step closer to getting out of town.

Just then Allie came in the kitchen wearing her swimsuit and flip-flops and carrying her backpack and beach towel. I started to laugh. "What have you got there?" She looked down at herself and then back at me. "I figure we're going to the beach."

"Close," I said. "But you're going to need more clothes than that to ride on an airplane."

And she was off again.

Next, I picked up the phone and called the airline. I booked three totally overpriced tickets and thanked the woman for robbing me blind. I didn't care. I wanted to do this. My family needed this.

I finished getting the little ones packed and then myself. As I loaded the car, the kids were talking ninety miles a minute. Oh, and the pleading. "Please, Mommy, tell us where we're going. Please, please, please."

"You'll find out soon enough," I kept telling them.

I took the box of recipes out of my car and carried it in the house like it was a carton of eggs. I even thought for a minute that now would be a good time to own a fire proof safe. But since we didn't, I had to trust that my house wouldn't burn to the ground before I got back. Because when we got back, my next project would be to decide just what to do with them. How was I going to make the best use of them?—besides the obvious? I didn't want to think about any of that now. For the moment I was putting everything else aside and spending the next few days just me and the kids. My mom had been right—I needed to get my shit together—if for no other reason than so my kids wouldn't grow up to be serial killers.

We pulled into the airport and Chase and Allie could hardly stand it. The suspense seemed to be killing them. They were so anxious, wondering where we were going. As soon as the attendant asked, "Destination?" and I said, "Orlando," Chase yelled out, "Disneyworld! We're going to Disneyworld!" And then the two of them danced around and were applauded by the people in line behind us. I hadn't seen them this happy in a long time. Why hadn't I done this sooner?

ఞ   ఞ   ఞ

I was wrong about Lucy. She never called me back. This worried me. I tried not to think about it while on the trip. I wanted to give my full attention to the kids. But on the plane ride home, it was all I could think about. I looked over at the Chase and Allie. They were sound asleep. Those poor babies stayed in high gear for four days and were completely exhausted. I must admit I was tired too. I don't remember being this tired in a long time. You would think that because I jog everyday I could handle anything, but there was something about Disneyworld that completely wiped me out. Maybe it was too much stimulation. We must have walked hundreds of miles over the last few days and eaten more cotton candy than one person should, but it was the best thing that could have happened for us. We all needed a break from reality.

We pulled into our driveway and I carried both kids into the house. They had managed to wake up long enough to get off the plane and walk to the car. Then they fell right back to sleep on the drive home. I lay them in their beds, removed their shoes and kissed them goodnight. It was only six o'clock in the evening. My head was pounding and my body ached. I decided unpacking the bags could wait until morning. I poured a glass of wine and went to my bathroom and ran the water in the tub. I stripped off my clothes and put on a robe. I went back to the kitchen to grab the wine bottle (I planned on being in the tub a long time) when there was a tapping on the back door. It startled me. I tied my robe around me a little tighter and went to see who was at the door. I nearly died. It was Drew and when he saw me, he smiled. I wanted so badly to pretend I didn't see him there, but it was kind of obvious—since we were looking right at each other through the glass.

I opened the door and let him in. He leaned forward like he was going to kiss me and I moved away. "What are you doing here?"

He looked puzzled. "I came to see you. I tried calling you but didn't get an answer."

Yeah, I saw that he called. I just ignored it.

"Look, Drew. This really isn't a good idea—you being here." I opened the door for him to leave but he didn't budge.

"But I broke it off with Lucy. I told her it wasn't working out."

My heart sank. "You did what?"

"Don't worry, she took it fine. She said she felt the same way."

My mind started racing. Oh, God, Lucy. He had broken her heart and it was my fault. I had to get him out of here—and fast.

"You've got to go, Drew."

"But I thought we could, you know, see where this is going."

I almost started laughing. Where did he think this was going? "Drew, I'm sorry. I think you misunderstood me. I wasn't looking for a relationship with you. I just wanted to have sex with you. And I did. And now it's over."

Drew's mouth fell open. "Are you fucking kidding me?" I thought he was about to cry.

"No, I'm not." I said as I held the door open wider.

"What am I supposed to do now?" he asked as he inched towards the door.

"Go back to California?" I said, trying my best not to be a smart ass.

Drew kissed me on the cheek and walked out the door. He turned once more and said, "You women are brutal."

Then I shut the door and locked it. And then I remembered—the bath was still running. Holy Shit!

Chapter 6

I walked in the bakery with the box of recipes. I couldn't wait to show everyone. I wanted us to try some of them—change up the menu a bit. I looked around for Lucy but Celia said she was running late. I was anxious to see her and dreaded seeing her—all at the same time. I had butterflies swimming in my stomach. Why hadn't she called me back? I'd left her several messages over the past few days and—nothing. It wasn't like her to not return my calls. We normally talked on the phone at least twice every day. I was worried she knew about Drew and me and that she wasn't speaking to me. I could hardly say I blamed her. I just hoped she was.

As Ben and Maria and I sat at a table reading through the faded pieces of paper, Lucy waltzed through the back door. I jumped out of my seat and nearly fell down getting to her. She greeted me with a "Howdy, Sis," and hung up her bag on the rack.

"Hey Lucy," I said. "Um, what's new?" My body switched into high alert mode. I slowly began to feel out of control of my actions. I had to fight the urge to blurt out *don't hate me but I slept with your boyfriend.* For a moment I thought about covering my mouth with my hand to keep that very thing from happening.

"Not a lot," she started. Then she turned to me. She put her hands on her hips and looked me square in the face. "Drew and I broke up."

There it was. She said it. I tried to act natural—but not too natural. What was I to do? How was I supposed to take this news? Should I act sad?—or happy? Confused? Pissed off? Relieved? What?

So I opted for, "Oh, Lucy. I'm sorry. What happened?" That was the best I could come up with.

She stared deeper into my eyes and said, "I think he was sleeping with someone else."

My heart did a nosedive into my stomach. My knees turned to jell-o.

"Who?" My voice cracked.

"You," She said matter-of-factly.

Wait. Did she just stick an *actual* knife in my chest or did it just feel like it?

I started to cry. "I'm so sorry, Lucy. I didn't mean for it to happen. I don't know what came over me—I really don't. You have to believe me that I never intended for this to happen. It just did. One minute we were arguing and the next minute…"

"OK, OK," she said, as she put her hand up to stop me from saying anything else. "I don't need the play by play." She then folded her arms across her chest. I still couldn't quite read her. Was she mad at me?

"You gotta know, Lucy, I know I'm the worst sister in the history of sisters."

Lucy unfolded her arms and put her hands on both my shoulders. When she did, I winced. I guess I thought she was going to hit me.

"You're not the worst sister—you're just horny."

When she said this we both laughed. And then I started to cry again. "Will you ever forgive me?"

"I already have."

I wiped my eyes on my apron and asked, "Where have you been and why haven't you called me back?"

"Oh, I went to San Antonio for the weekend. I met someone."

I shook my head in disbelief. "Why does that not surprise me?"

Lucy turned the conversation back to me. "So are you and Drew going to get married?" She was making fun of me now.

"No. I told him to go back to California."

Her mouth opened. "You did?"

"Yes. You were right, I was just horny."

And as I turned to walk away, Lucy popped me with a towel on my behind.

ଓଟ   ଓଟ   ଓଟ

Later that morning, Mrs. Sugarman called and I answered the phone. She placed an order and told me someone would be in later to pick it up. I was surprised she wasn't coming in herself because I quite enjoy our chats together. I asked if she was feeling well and she assured she was—just a little under the weather. We hung up the phone and I realized how much I'd come to care about her. She reminded me of my mother in a lot of ways. I wondered why I hadn't thought of that before.

I showed Lucy the box of recipes I'd found in our parents' attic and she seemed as excited as I was. She pulled out three or four that she liked and started to work on them. Our plan was to mix up a batch of several new things—the walnut fudge brownies, the blueberry cream cheese muffins, the chocolate chess tartlets, the chocolate mint pound cake and the pumpkin chess pie—and see what our customers said about them.

There was an air of excitement in the bakery. Everyone seemed almost giddy. It was like opening presents at Christmas. I thought about how lucky I was to have these people working with me—people who were just as passionate about food as me.

Around two o'clock, the kitchen was busy. Lucy was on the phone with a guy who designs websites. She had the idea to start an online ordering site that would expand our customer base. I had to admit I was quite impressed. Everyone else was busy mixing, stirring, chopping and baking. I sat with my laptop in front of me and had begun the tedious task of typing all the recipes on Word documents so that we could read them better and so I wouldn't have to worry about losing them. The thought of that made me shiver.

The door chimed and I got up from my desk and headed to the front. Standing at the counter was a handsome man I'd never seen before. He was wearing a beautiful black suit (if I had to guess I'd say it was Zegna—Bryan owned several just like this one) and Gucci loafers— definitely Gucci. His hair was dark and had just enough gray to make him look distinguished—not old. When he noticed me, he smiled.

I asked, "Can I help you?"

"Yes. I'm here to pick up an order for my grandmother and I was given specific instructions to only talk to Claire."

"You must be Mrs. Sugarman's grandson."

"Claire?" He asked.

"Guilty." I tried not to sound too desperate or too ridiculous.

He stuck out his hand to shake mine. "Henry Sugarman."

"It's nice to meet you." I took my hand from his and wiped it on my apron. Why did I do that? He saw me do it too. I was so embarrassed. What was wrong with me? The moment became suddenly awkward. And then there was silence. Neither one of us said anything for what seemed like minutes—even though it had only been a few seconds.

"Oh," I finally said. "Your grandmother's order is ready. Let me get it."

I disappeared to the back and gave myself a talking to. *Pull yourself together, you lunatic!*

I grabbed her order and carried it to the front. I handed him the box and when I did, our hands touched. I was afraid I might start giggling. He was *really* handsome—and definitely not in his twenties. I tried to be charming. "Please tell your grandmother I hope she feels better."

He seemed confused. "Grandmother? She's fine. She's sailing on the lake today."

Why that little faker.

"Oh, is she now? I must have misunderstood. Well, send her my best."

Henry turned to leave. "I will. Thank you again."

"Goodbye. Come back anytime." Could I sound more pathetic?

"I will. I never knew this place was here before. I like it. It's very charming."

And he waved as he walked out the door. I stood there for a minute watching him walk to his car.

"What a loser." Lucy said from behind me.

I turned towards her and snapped, "He's not a loser."

"I was talking about you. You have absolutely no game," Lucy said as she shook her head at me.

"Excuse me, but I'm out of practice. We don't *all* have as much experience as you."

"That's true," she said as she began filling the case with more sugar cookies.

"But by the way you were acting you might have had better luck with him if you'd taken off your shirt and flashed your boobs."

I grabbed a towel and began wiping down the counter. "Don't be so vulgar, Lucy. It's not easy for me. I didn't want this. I didn't want to be single and putting myself out there. I was married—*happily* married. Nothing about this is what I wanted. So excuse me if I don't exactly know what the hell I'm doing."

She picked up the last cookie from the sheet and popped it in her mouth. "You're right. I'm sorry. I guess it didn't help that I slept with your boyfriend. Oh wait!—that was you."

I stopped wiping, threw the towel on the ground and ran toward her. She let out a scream and started running. I chased her around the store until I caught her—the whole time she was laughing and squealing. Ben and the others came to the front and watched as the two of us ran around like ten year olds. I finally caught Lucy, tackled her to the ground and lay on top of her, tickling her silly. The front door opened just then and we stopped, looked up and saw Henry Sugarman standing over us. I tried to get off the floor gracefully, but really, how was that possible?

He seemed a little surprised to find us on the floor. I'd never been so embarrassed—well, except for a few minutes ago when he was in here the *first* time.

"Hi again. I'm sorry to interrupt you while you're…um, obviously very busy… but I was driving around the block trying to get up the nerve to invite you to dinner."

My heart did a back flip. I smoothed my hair back and tried my best not to gush. "Sure—that would be great."

Lucy was still standing there so Henry extended his hand and introduced himself. I'm sure it was awkward for him—asking me out in front of an audience. The others went back inside the kitchen. Then Lucy, still shaking his hand, said to Henry, "Would you excuse us for just a minute? I need to borrow Claire."

I gave Lucy a questioning look and then smiled at Henry. "I'll be right back."

I followed Lucy to the kitchen. Everyone had gone back to what they were doing before all the excitement.

"What is it, Lucy?" She was beginning to irritate me. Henry was standing out there waiting for me. I had to get back before he changed his mind about wanting to take me to dinner.

"I think you should play hard to get," she said, obviously trying not to laugh. And then she added, "oh, and don't sleep with him until *after* he's paid the check. Be a slut—but not *too* slutty."

Great. Now I was getting dating advice from the world's oldest adolescent.

I turned and stomped out of the kitchen, but not before yelling, "Idiot!" in her direction. I found Henry at the counter, sampling the chocolate chess tartlets we'd put out.

"Mmmm. These are really delicious." He said as he grabbed another one.

"Thank you. Take as many as you like."

So he did just that. He stood there, paying no attention to me, eating tartlet after tartlet.

Someone had to say something. "So you were saying something about dinner?"

Henry turned to me like he just remembered why he was there.

"Yes, sorry." He licked the chocolate from his fingers. "Is Friday good for you?"

"Friday's great." I wrote my address on a piece of paper and handed it to him.

"Seven o'clock OK?" He asked, still eyeing the tartlets.

"Seven's fine," I said. He seemed to be quite taken with the sweets. "Would you like some of those to go?"

He turned to me and smiled. "Yes, I'd love some."

Chapter 7

I was shaking so badly I couldn't put my lipstick on straight. I paced the room, telling myself this was no big deal. It was just dinner—with a man. Yeah, that's right. Just two people who would be sitting at the same table at the same time, having a meal. I mean everyone has to eat, right? I walked into Bryan's closet and took in a deep breath through my nose. I could still smell him. It was faint and I had to really concentrate, but it was there. I touched his shirts, still hung neatly in a row—all color coordinated. That was just like him. His whole life was organized down to his dress socks. He was the complete opposite of me.

I remember the first time Bryan and I went out. I was living in an apartment on the Westside—the cultural part of town. We met at a party through mutual friends and exchanged phone numbers. He called the next day and sounded so nervous on the phone that he stumbled over his words. I had to cover my mouth not to laugh out loud. He finally got out the words "can I take you to dinner?" and I was going to jack with him, but thought better of it. The poor guy sounded like he was on the verge of a breakdown. Instead I accepted his offer and he let out an audible sigh. I guess he'd been holding his breath.

When he arrived at my apartment he was *way* more adorable than I'd remembered from the party—tall, sandy blonde hair, brown eyes, impeccable dresser. His hands must have been sweaty because the entire ride to the restaurant he kept wiping them on his pants. The whole night the conversation flowed and even the silent moments were comfortable. Dinner lingered on until the restaurant was nearly empty. We talked about everything from politics to college football. When we finally left the restaurant, he drove me home, kissed me goodnight, and I knew then I would marry him. Six months later, he proposed.

I looked at the clock. Henry would be there any minute. I put on my dress, slipped on my sling backs and rechecked myself in the mirror for the millionth time. I still looked good—no, I looked great—not a day over thirty-five if I did say so myself. I practiced smiling. I practiced laughing. I needed to do this more. I'm much prettier when I smile—but I hadn't had much to smile about lately. I took another deep breath. Then the doorbell rang. I could feel the butterflies begin to swarm in my stomach.

It wasn't Henry. It was the babysitter, Lizzy. I gave her instructions, called Pizza Hut, and then raced to my room to check myself in the mirror once more. I was beginning to sweat. I sprayed a little more perfume, ratted my hair just enough to give the appearance that I was taller than my five-foot-four frame, and sat down on the edge of my bed. And I waited. Ten minutes passed. Twenty minutes passed. I checked the clock—seven thirty. Had he gotten lost? Was I wrong about the day? He'd said Friday, right? It was Friday. Wait. Was it Friday?

I ran to the TV room (which wasn't easy to do in heels) where the kids were and said, "Lizzy, it's Friday, isn't it?"

Lizzy looked from the TV to me and said, "Yeah, Friday."

OK, there was no need to panic. He was just running late. I went to my cell phone—no missed calls. I picked up the land line—it wasn't off the hook. I went to the front room and looked out the window onto the street. There were no cars coming. I paced the room for ten minutes when finally—a car pulled up to the house. I looked out the window only to find that it was only the goddamned pizza delivery boy. I nearly broke down. He rang the bell. I paid the kid, tossed the pizza on the table, and then went to my room and shut the door.

What an idiot I'd been. I let myself get excited about going on a date—with a seemingly decent guy—and he stood me up. I couldn't call him—I didn't get his number. I'm not sure I would have anyway. As I stripped off my clothes and wiped the makeup off my face, I wondered why he hadn't shown up. Had he changed his mind? If so, why? Am I that unlovable?

A few minutes later, I sent Lizzy home. She seemed confused. I told her my plans had changed and that I wouldn't be going out after all. She grabbed a couple more slices of pizza and left. I joined the kids in the family room and fell asleep on the couch watching The Incredibles.

CB CB CB

On Monday, the bakery was hopping. Word was spreading about the new items on our menu and we were slammed with orders. Ben suggested we hire more help. The mood in the kitchen was tense— everyone was busy and at times we were anxious and short with each other. I felt a little overwhelmed—but in a good way. It was hectic, but it was also great. It's what I'd wanted. Lucy asked me how my date went and I told her it didn't happen. I could tell she wanted to press me for more information, but the phone kept ringing and I was grateful we were both distracted. I'd thought about Henry all weekend and made up all kinds of reasons why he hadn't shown up. The one I kept telling myself was that he must have died in a car wreck on the way to pick me up. I know that was grossly morbid, but it worked. By Monday, I didn't seem to care so much.

We had so many more deliveries than normal that Maria and Celia had to use their own cars. Lucy just couldn't do them all herself. Ben suggested we get another van and I agreed to give it some thought. I wasn't exactly ready for all this. The bakery was beginning to boom and it was happening so fast—too fast. I was afraid I couldn't do it. Everyone, including me, was excited and nervous about the surge in business. We'd never been so busy. And we were going to give it our best shot. I owed it to everyone to make this work and I especially owed it to myself. Bryan would be so proud of me. But he'd also know what to tell me to do. It was hard making all the decisions on my own. So I didn't. I found myself relying more and more on Ben. He'd become my go-to guy. I would be at home some nights and have an idea and call him—sometimes waking him up. I found myself needing him more all the time.

After lunch I was scrolling through the recipes, looking for the next big thing. All the new items we'd introduced were big hits—especially the chocolate chess tartlets and the chocolate mint pound cake. We couldn't keep those things in the store. Ben was on me to come up with something else so that's what I'd been trying to do all day. I was glad to have a manager like him. He practically single-handedly ran the kitchen. Correction—he *did* single-handedly run the kitchen.

Maria came back to where I was sitting and said, "There's someone out there to see you."

I got up from behind the desk and went to the front. Henry was there, sampling the blueberry cream cheese muffins. I immediately felt queasy and my heart started to race.

He looked at me, but he didn't smile. He looked upset.

"Hello, Henry." I tried not to let my disappointment show.

"Claire. Listen, I'm sorry about the other night. I should have called, but…"

"Look, it's OK," I interrupted. "You don't owe me an explanation."

"No, you don't understand. My grandmother passed away unexpectedly Friday afternoon. And things were chaotic after that."

My heart sank. I got tears in my eyes thinking about Mrs. Sugarman. "I'm so sorry, Henry. Are you OK? What happened?"

"We don't exactly know. She had been feeling fine. There was nothing unusual about her mood. The staff said she had lunch in the dining room like she always does. Then she told them she was going to her room to lie down—which wasn't out of the ordinary for her. Then around five the night maid went to tell her dinner was ready and she couldn't wake her."

I went to him and put my arms around him. I don't know what possessed me to do it—it just seemed like the right thing to do. Although it was kind of weird since I barely knew the man. I tried to pull away and he held me tighter for a minute longer. It was incredible—and weird.

When we finally broke free from one another, Henry reached in his coat pocket and pulled out an envelope. He handed it to me and said, "The maid found this letter on her desk. It's addressed to you."

That was odd. Why would she write me a letter? I tore open the seal and unfolded the piece of paper. It was short. It was just two sentences. And it read:

Claire,

You are stronger than you think. You can handle a heaping spoonful.

Rose Sugarman

I held the letter to my chest and broke down crying. Henry looked worried and asked, "What does it say?"

I handed it to him and he read it out loud. He then looked at me and asked, "What does it mean?"

I stopped crying for a minute, wiped my eyes on my apron, and said, "I think it means I need to get off my ass and stop feeling sorry for myself."

Henry looked confused. He read the letter once more and handed it back to me. I smiled up at him. Just then he leaned down, kissed me gently on the lips and asked, "Do you want to go with me to the house?"

I went from being sad, to shocked, to excited, to confused, to sad again.

I nodded my head, took off my apron and left for the Sugarman estate.

Ↄ   Ↄ   Ↄ

We pulled up to the house and I was speechless. I'd never seen anything so magnificent before. I mean, I'd heard stories about what this place looked like, but no one's descriptions came remotely close to doing it justice. Pecan trees lined the drive up to the house. In the middle of the sprawling green lawn was a small lake filled with black and white swan. Bright red crepe myrtles and magnolia trees surrounded the main house which looked larger than most hotels in Dallas. OK, I might have been exaggerating a little, but it was massive. We parked the car and walked toward the front door. The entrance was intimidating with its marble pillars and mahogany doors. Several delivery trucks and floral vans sat in the driveway, plus about twenty more Mercedes, Porches and Limos. Once inside, I looked around at the beauty that lay before me. The floors were dark, hand-scraped red oak, the ceilings so high I wondered how they changed the light bulbs. The house was in full swing. Flowers were being placed throughout the main foyer and sitting room, the staff busy sprucing up the place like they were getting ready for a party. Bartenders were mixing drinks and butlers were serving hors d'oeuvres. Henry motioned for me to follow him. We entered what I assumed to be the library. It was filled floor to ceiling with books, pictures in frames, and massive furniture. He went to the bar and reached for a couple of glasses. After putting ice in them, he poured in vodka, soda and squeezed a couple of limes.

He brought the glasses over to where I was standing and handed one to me. He held out his glass, we clinked them together and he said, "To Grandmother."

After downing the first of two drinks, my head began swimming and my eyes blurred a little. We left the room and found more people starting to arrive. I felt a little out of place in my jeans and Heaping Spoonful t-shirt. I looked around at the men—they were in black suits—the women in high fashion pant suits and dresses. I looked down at myself and Henry must have sensed my uneasiness because he placed his hand on the small of my back, leaned in and whispered, "You look great."

His touch made me quiver a little and I wondered if it was bad form to think about him naked. I talked with fifty people I didn't know—a few of them city officials and most of them, millionaires. I excused myself to the ladies room. I looked in the mirror and was horrified by what I saw. My hair, which had been neatly pulled back earlier, was messy and my eye makeup smeared from crying. How could Henry think I looked great? I was beginning to question his taste in women.

I did my best to compose myself—at least so I wouldn't look like I'd just rolled out of bed—and headed towards the crowd of people again. One woman stopped me and asked if I was the caterer. I shook my head and let her know I was actually a guest of Henry. She, in her couture looking white linen dress suit, raised an eyebrow and proceeded to look me up and down. Just then, Henry came up, excused the both of us and we escaped out the back door. Wow. The back of the house was even more amazing than the front. The lawn went on for miles and it was covered in apple and pear trees. Henry pointed to an area on the left that displayed Mrs. Sugarman's rose garden. He said she was an avid gardener. I smiled. I never knew that about her. Apparently there was a lot I didn't know. As we walked the grounds, Henry told me how his grandmother had been one of the first city council members in Dallas. She held places on boards all over town, including the orphanage, the women's shelter, the public school board (although her own children went to private school) and the children's hospital. Her whole life had been spent helping other people. She was filthy rich and spent her time finding ways to give her money to people who needed it and causes she believed in. As he was talking, I felt a real peace about everything. And I realized something also—she'd been helping me all along and I didn't recognize it. She believed in me. And I owed it to her to believe in myself.

Once back inside, we noticed the crowd had dwindled down to a few. I knew it must be late in the day, so I phoned my dad, told him where I was, and asked him to get the children from Ana. After we hung up, I turned to find Henry signaling for me to join him in the kitchen. I slipped through the door and closed it behind me. There, on the table, was a beautiful spread—spiral ham, roasted new potatoes, dill carrots, spinach salad, and homemade dinner rolls (from my bakery, of course). He pulled out the chair for me and as I sat down asked, "What is all this?"

"Well," Henry said, "It seems that I owe you dinner." He smiled at me and placed a napkin in his lap.

We ate and talked and were only interrupted twice—once by the lady in the white dress suit who was looking for the wine—and once by a maid who came over and poured more water. It was a lovely dinner (given the circumstances) and I really enjoyed spending time with him. There was easiness about him—much like Bryan. He was gentle and seemed to have a good heart. He was close to his family. He certainly loved his grandmother.

It was dark before we left. I called my dad to check on Chase and Allie. They were begging to spend the night and he said he wanted the company. I covered the phone with my hand and asked Henry, "Do you have plans?"

He raised an eyebrow and said, "I do now."

Instead of taking me to my car, I asked Henry to swing by my house so I could change clothes. He pulled up to the house and together we went inside. I walked toward the bedroom and yelled behind me, "Make yourself at home. There's wine in the fridge."

I hurriedly undressed, gave myself a spit bath, and dressed in pants and a blouse. I took my hair down, brushed it out, and did my best to make it do something. I reapplied makeup, brushed my teeth, and spritzed myself with Vera Wang's fragrance. Satisfied, I joined Henry in the kitchen and when he saw me did a double take.

"Wow. You look amazing."

I couldn't help but blush. "Thank you. You're not so bad yourself."

He poured me a glass of wine and we stood there for a minute, sipping in silence.

I was the first to speak. "What do you want to do?" I asked.

"Besides kiss you right now?"

OK, I was giddy. I felt like I was in middle school all over again. A chill ran from the bottom of my spine, all the way to the top of my head. I stood there, grinning like an idiot.

"You want to kiss me?"

"Uh-huh," he said as he took the glass from my hand and wrapped his arms around me. I closed my eyes as he moved closer to me. He put his lips on mine and it felt...well, it was awesome.

We kissed and we kissed and I never wanted to stop. He finally pulled away and said, "That was really nice."

I still had my eyes closed. It *was* nice. And desperately needed.

Chapter 8

The service was held at St. Stephen's Episcopal Church downtown. The place was packed. The pews filled up quickly and the rest of the congregation had to stand. There were so many different kinds of people there: from city officials, like the mayor, to doctors, police officers and, of course, her entire staff. Even the governor of Texas attended. It was amazing—the turnout. She had affected so many people's lives. Henry insisted I sit with the family, although I felt a little out of place. I mean, I had only met him a few days earlier and we were still getting to know each other. His parents, his aunts, uncles and cousins were kind to me and I tried to remember the names of everyone I met. It was a little overwhelming. As the priest welcomed everyone to the service, Henry reached over and grabbed my hand and held it. When he did the butterflies danced around inside my stomach again. I closed my eyes and thought back to the night we spent, snuggled on the sofa in my living room, sharing secrets and telling stories, laughing, and drinking wine. It had been amazing—and so comfortable—like we'd known each other for a million years. I know people say that all the time, but it was true. Kissing was as far as we'd gotten in the intimacy department. I had already decided I wasn't going to jump into bed with him too quickly. I wanted to do this the right way. I shared my feelings with Henry and he seemed to understand. As the sun was coming up, we realized we'd been talking all night. Not able to fight sleep any longer, each of us lay our head on the back of the sofa and fell asleep, our bodies entwined.

Over the next few weeks, Henry and I started getting closer. We still hadn't made love, but had become familiar with each other in different ways. He took me to dinner, he hung out at the bakery when I worked late, and we went to the movies. I decided it was time to introduce him to Chase and Allie. I was hesitant at first because I'd never done anything like this. I cooked dinner and invited him over. I was afraid of their reaction, but was surprised at how much they liked Henry—although, I shouldn't have been *that* surprised. He had an easy way about him. He was not commanding of attention and he spoke in a rather gentle voice. Henry asked Chase about sports and super heroes (Superman is his favorite and the greatest all-time super hero in his young opinion). He sat on the floor in Allie's room and let her put clips in his hair and makeup on his face. I stood in the doorway watching this, feeling happier than I had in a long time. He and I exchanged glances and he seemed to be comfortable with all of it.

Later, when we said goodbye, I realized I hadn't thought of Bryan that day—not until just then—and my thought was this: Bryan would really like Henry. They might have even been friends.

CB   CB   CB

I'd been thinking, with the help of Henry, about compiling all the recipes into a cookbook, along with the history of the recipes, and try to get it published. I'd never considered this before, but my recent visits with my mother had sparked the idea. She had been telling me stories— her family's fascinating history—and their struggle to get to the United States from Germany. My great-great-grandmother had baked cakes and breads and sold them to the locals in her small town, trying to save enough money to move her family. My great-great grandfather had died from polio and left my great-great grandmother to care for their seven children and their elders. She took up with a wealthy man who had a sweet tooth (not only for her cooking, but for her) and a better equipped kitchen. She never shared with him her plans to move her family to the U.S. She just kept baking and cooking until she'd raised enough money to flee. She eventually managed to get everyone on a ship and they headed west. She also unexpectedly brought with her child number eight—my great grandfather, who it turns out, really was a bastard.

I told Henry all of this—how she was so colorful in her descriptions and how she seemed to have every single detail down to the smallest. It seemed her mother and her mother's mother worked hard to preserve the stories. And it was about to stop with my mother unless I did something about it. That's when he suggested I take a recorder with me, so I could get the details right. So I did. She told the stories like they happened yesterday. And telling them always made her eyes sparkle. At times she was so animated that I would laugh out loud, only to cover my mouth so that my voice wouldn't record over her tales. My favorite story involved my great grandfather, Harry, and his cousin, Oscar. One summer, Grandpa Harry had a job at an amusement park called Casino Beach. He did everything from sweep up the trash to retrieve the balls from under the miniature golf course. Grandpa Harry's mother was very strict and gave him instructions to be home no later than 10:15 every night. She warned him that if he ever broke curfew there would be trouble. The park closed at ten so that gave him exactly fifteen minutes to walk home—which was plenty of time. One day, his cousin, Oscar, spent the night and went to work with him. Before they left for the park, his mother reminded them to be home on time. After his shift was over, my great grandfather and his cousin took a detour home and ended up at the lake. They spent more than a half hour there throwing rocks, seeing who was better at skipping them across the water. They knew they were late and were probably going to get into trouble when they finally got home. But still they didn't hurry. They walked at a leisurely pace, talking the whole time about Susan Summers and her blonde, curly hair. My grandfather thought she was the most beautiful girl in the world. And she didn't know he existed. Oscar teased him, calling him the Invisible Man. Grandpa Harry punched him in the arm and they both laughed. Once they got to their street, they stood outside the house, daring each other in go in first. Finally my great grandfather said to his cousin, "you go in first. She won't do anything to you—you're not her son. You won't get licks. Go on, check to see if the coast is clear, then come back and tell me—but be quiet." Oscar hesitated at first, but then reasoned that his aunt probably wouldn't punish him. So he tiptoed onto the front porch and opened the door very slowly and disappeared inside. A few seconds later he came running out the house as fast as he could, screaming bloody murder, "She's behind the door, *she's behind the door!*" Grandpa Harry laughed as he watched Oscar run across the field, the full moon shining on him in the night sky. Grandpa Harry's mom came out on the front porch and was laughing herself. She had been waiting behind the door with a switch in her hand, waiting for them to get home. When Oscar came into the house, she gave him a lashing on his behind. Needless to say, it was a long time before Oscar stayed the night there again. And Grandpa Harry never broke curfew again.

It was a great time for us—and I began to appreciate the recipes I'd been given more than ever. I felt a real need to protect them and to somehow share them with the world. And that's just what I was going to do.

⚃ ⚃ ⚃

The bakery was busier than ever. I did buy another van and I did hire more help. I continued to lean on Ben. He and I had become such great friends—even outside of work. A few times a week we grabbed dinner together, and once he helped Chase with his science project. He seemed to go on lots of first dates, but there was no one serious in his life. I assumed it was because he worked all the time. It couldn't have been because he wasn't handsome or that he wasn't a nice guy. I was selfishly grateful that he didn't have someone special in his life. I needed him to help me with the business. I felt very safe with him around. He seemed to take on the store as if it were his own. I couldn't have asked for anything more. Celia and Maria were taking on more managerial roles, teaching the new employees everything they needed to know and coordinating the delivery schedules. Lucy took charge of the online orders—which seemed to be a full time job now. It was crazy how fast the business was growing. Sometimes Ben and I would be there well into the night, taking inventory, ordering supplies, and baking extra batches of everything. We'd order pizza and Ben would run to the convenience store and grab a six pack of beer. He would tell exaggerated stories (I assumed he was exaggerating) of single life and dating in Dallas. It sounded awful—and brutal. Because of his busy work schedule, he didn't have a lot of time to go out and meet people. So he resorted to online dating. One girl he met on the internet didn't have a picture on her profile, so he thought there was a fifty-fifty shot that she might not be attractive, but she sounded really nice. He took a chance and met her at a restaurant. She showed up, and was cute enough, until she opened her mouth. That's when he noticed she only had one tooth in her entire mouth. He was speechless. Because he is such a nice guy he didn't want to be rude and ditch her, so he bought her dinner. She ordered soup—and he couldn't help but stare at her toothless mouth as she ate—or tried to eat. He told me it was the longest hour and a half of his life. When I heard this I laughed so hard I thought I might pee my pants. If this was work, it sure didn't feel like it.

With my busier schedule, my dad took on a bigger role with my kids. The nights I stayed late at the bakery he would relieve Ana, cook dinner for them, get them ready for bed and read books to them until I got home. Not always being there for them made me feel guilty, but they seemed to really enjoy the time with their grandfather. And it was great for my dad as well. He seemed happier and less lonely. At least that's what I told myself to keep the feelings of guilt from completely taking over my body.

Henry would join us for dinner on the nights I was home and he and the children seemed to be forming a real friendship. He regularly brought them treats and I would playfully scold him—claiming he was going to spoil them. We were all getting used to the idea of having him around.

I found that I smiled a lot more these days and Lucy noticed, too. She came into the bakery one morning and said, "Looks like someone's getting laid regularly."

I scoffed, "Well don't look at me." And then I whispered, "Henry and I haven't had sex yet."

She looked mortified. She screamed, "Why not?"

"Because (as if it's any of your business), we want to wait."

This seemed to puzzle Lucy even more. "Why?"

I looked at her for a minute, not really knowing the answer, and before I could think of one she said, "Oh, I get it. He's gay."

Well, I'd just about heard it all. "He's not gay, you idiot!"

I said this a little too loudly because everyone in the kitchen stopped and turned to face me.

I took Lucy by the arm and led her out the back door.

"I just don't want to rush into anything. I don't want to jinx it."

Lucy shook her head as if this was the most ridiculous thing she'd ever heard. "Hopeless—that's what you are—completely hopeless."

"Fuck off," I said as I opened the door, went inside and left her standing there, still shaking her head.

C3   CB   CB

A few days later, I woke up in the morning with a terrible pain in my stomach. I felt I was going to be sick, so I rushed to the bathroom and barely made it to the toilet. I heaved and heaved until there was nothing left. I wiped my mouth with a towel that was folded over the tub, and went to stand up. I immediately fell to my knees in pain. My stomach ached so badly that I couldn't get up—the pain so sharp it felt like I'd been stabbed. I looked down between my legs and saw blood coming from underneath my gown. Panicked, I crawled back to the bedroom and called my dad. I told him something was wrong. He told me to hang up and dial 9-1-1 and I agreed, but when I turned off the receiver, I dialed Lucy's number instead. I screamed at her to hurry and come get me. I didn't want to call 9-1-1 and have an ambulance come. That would have freaked out my kids. I didn't want them to know something was wrong—they would worry too much. I just couldn't do that to them.

I lay on the bathroom floor waiting for Lucy. In the meantime I heard Ana come in the front door. I yelled for her, but she must not have heard me because she never came. After what seemed like forever, I finally heard Lucy's voice call out, "Claire, Claire."

"I'm in the bathroom." I screamed.

She looked at me and her eyes widened. "Where's the blood coming from?"

"My vagina, I think."

"When was your last period?" she asked as she began helping me off the floor. I was still doubled over in pain.

"I don't know? What does that have to do with anything?" What was she talking about? Wait. When *was* my last period?

"I think you're having a miscarriage," Lucy said as she put a towel between my legs and helped me down the hallway.

"A miscarriage? How could I be having a miscarriage? I haven't had se…"

And then I remembered. I had had sex—with Drew—about six weeks ago. Holy shit—I *was* having a miscarriage.

I immediately started to sob and Ana looked worried as she watched Lucy help me out the door. Lucy turned and said to Ana over her shoulder, "We'll call you in a little while. Don't say anything to the kids." Ana nodded in agreement. I couldn't say anything. I was in complete shock.

At the hospital, I was taken back right away. Apparently there's no waiting if you're bleeding from your crotch. The doctor rushed in after a few minutes and began asking question after question and pressing on my abdomen. He agreed with Lucy that I was probably having a miscarriage, but was going to order an ultrasound and do blood work to be certain.

I was so worried—so distraught. What would Henry think? Would I have to tell him? What would I say? How would I explain this? I hadn't been completely honest with him about everything—but in my defense I kind of forgot the whole "Drew" thing. I didn't even remember it when the conversation came up with Henry. I told him I hadn't had sex with anyone since Bryan died. And I think a part of me believed that. But, if he finds out about this, he'll know I lied. Then he may wonder if I've lied about other things. This was not good. I closed my eyes and cried big, salty tears. Lucy sat next to me, holding my hand, trying to comfort me. She kept saying, "I'm so sorry, I'm so sorry," and I wondered what she had to be sorry for. I had done this all by myself. The day that Drew and I had sex I never once thought about birth control. I wasn't used to having to. Bryan had a vasectomy when Allie was six months old and I hadn't worried about it since then. It amazed me how fucking stupid I could be sometimes.

The doctor came in a while later with the results of my blood work. I was pregnant. The ultrasound tech looked in my uterus and found a yolk sac—which meant there was a baby in my belly, but they weren't able to find a heartbeat. I was far enough along, they said, where there would have been one visible to the naked eye. They called it an incomplete miscarriage, meaning it hadn't extracted itself from my body yet. I was given two options: a) have a DNC where the doctor goes in and scrapes everything out of my uterus, or b) go home with lots of pain medicine and wait for it to happen naturally. I didn't like either of those options.

Just then my dad rushed in and Lucy pulled him outside and, I guess, filled him in. They returned a few minutes later and he came over to the side of the hospital bed and kissed me on the forehead. I looked in his face—he had tears in his eyes. This made everything so much worse. I couldn't tell if he was worried, sad, or disappointed. Maybe it was all of the above. I whispered, "I'm sorry Daddy."

"You're going to be all right," he said as he squeezed my shoulder and mustered a smile.

I panicked and said to both of them, "Do me a favor—don't say anything about this to Henry. Not until I figure out how to tell him or what to say."

My dad raised his hand up and said, "I already talked to him. I went to your house but you'd already gone when he called. I answered and said something was wrong—that I didn't know what, but that you were taken to the hospital. He's on his way up here. I'm sorry Claire."

Oh my God, Oh my God, Oh my God.

Chapter 9

When Henry rushed in to the room, Dad and Lucy looked at each other and seemed to be thinking the same thing—they split. Henry came to my side and put his hand on my forehead, moving the hair from my eyes. Upon seeing him, I broke down crying. My stomach was in knots and I had no idea what to say.

He was the first to speak. "What's the matter, Claire? What happened? I was so scared when your dad told me you were brought to the hospital."

I looked at him. He did look scared—and worried. I didn't know how I was going to get the words to come out of my mouth. I had to tell him. I had to take a chance and tell him the truth.

"Um, Henry. This is so hard to say but…" I stopped, took in a deep breath and let it out.

"What? What is it Claire? Are you OK? Are you sick?" Henry was sitting on the bed now, holding my hand.

I shook my head. "I'm not sick. I'm fine. I just had a..." I couldn't say it.

"A what?" Henry asked. He went from looking upset to unsure.

"I'm having a miscarriage." There. I said it. Please God, don't let him hate me.

"A miscarriage?" Henry looked at my stomach and then back at me. "But that's impossible. We haven't..." His voice trailed off. And then, "Oh, I see." He let go of my hand and stood up.

I rearranged myself so that I could sit up better. "See what? Henry, let me explain. I can explain this."

He held up a hand and waved me off. He looked at the ground and said, "No need Claire." He wouldn't look me in the face.

I started crying uncontrollably. "Henry, please. You don't understand."

"Oh I think I do. You didn't want to have sex with me because you were having sex somewhere else." He raised his voice for the first time since I'd met him. He looked hurt and his eyes were full of anger, his voice trembling. He was pissed. He hated me already.

"That's not it at all. Please Henry, sit down and let me talk to you." I was practically begging now.

My dad and Lucy came back into the room then. Henry saw them and said in my direction, "I can't do this. I won't do this." And then he walked out of the room and out of my life.

The next few days I spent recovering at home. I'd opted for plan b—waiting for my body to heal itself. I figured I deserved any pain that I was going to experience. I'd earned it. After a few more days I tried calling Henry several times but he never answered, never returned my calls. I had single-handedly fucked up our relationship and now he was gone. It didn't appear that he was going to forgive me. And I was distraught. The universe can be wicked.

When I finally returned to work, everyone stopped what they were doing when they saw me. Ugh. Lucy. I guessed she'd told them everything. I sat at my desk and pretended to be busy, but I could feel all of them staring at me. I tried my best to smile and act normal, but who the fuck knows what normal is anymore. I'd gone so far from normal that I didn't even know who I was anymore. Luckily my children didn't know what had happened. I told them it was "mommy" stuff—and Allie looked worried and said she didn't want to be a mommy. I kissed her cheek and assured her she would change her mind when she was older. My dad had been supportive—and Ana too. Everyone pitched in and helped me while I waited for my body to expel the remains of the baby that once lived inside me.

I had mixed emotions about the whole ordeal. Sure it cost me my relationship with Henry—that part sucked. But the thought of having another baby stirred up so many emotions for me. I thought I was finished having children—Bryan and I agreed—we had a boy and girl—a happy, complete family. But I couldn't help but feel sad about losing this child. In the end I chalked it up to bad timing. What's that saying? God never gives us more than we can handle? I guess he thinks I can handle a lot. Boy, do I have him snowed!

Ben came to where I was sitting and handed me a folder. "What's this? I asked.

"Open it up and see." He seemed proud of himself.

What I saw inside took my breath away. It was a mock up—a rough copy—of what our cookbook was going to look like. Lucy skipped over and chimed in, "We sent it to a publisher and this lady called us about it. She's really interested." Lucy could barely contain her excitement. Ben smiled and asked, "I hope you're not upset that we did all this without consulting you."

I was speechless. In front of me was page after page of my family's recipes, along with the stories my mother had told me. I had, over the last month, been painstakingly playing and replaying the recorder, typing the words as I heard them. Ben and Lucy had printed them off and put it all together. It was a wonderful surprise. Tears welled in my eyes. I closed the folder and placed my hand on top of it saying, "I needed this. Thank you."

Ben looked at Lucy and the two smiled at each other and then at me. Lucy leaned down and hugged my neck. "I love you, Claire," she said. I felt my heart begin to mend.

ᘓ ᘓ ᘓ

The cookbook came together quickly. Maria's husband was a graphic designer—he came up with the cover. I took pictures of my mother and of her family that I found in a box (where else?) in the attic in my parents' house and sent those along with recent photos of me, Lucy, my dad and the bakery. Seeing the finished product for the first time was one of the best days of my life. It was perfect—and I couldn't believe we had actually done it. I took it up to the nursing home to show to my mother. She wasn't having a good day. She kept calling me Dorothy—her sister's name, and repeated the words, "chocolate pudding, chocolate pudding," over and over. It upset me, seeing her this way. I tried getting her attention by saying, "Mother, it's me Claire," but it didn't work. She was staring out the window, completely oblivious to me. When I would try and get her to look at me she would say, "You're in my way, Dorothy."

I left there in tears. I was sad because I'd so wanted her to see what she'd inspired us to do. The cookbook was for her. I wanted her to be proud of it—of me—of herself. I was pulling out of the parking lot when my cell phone rang. I composed myself and answered. "Hello. Is this Claire Hamilton?—from Heaping Spoonful?"

"Yes," I answered.

"Ms. Hamilton, this is Roberta Collins from WDAL—the television station in Dallas. I'm wondering if I can talk to you for a minute."

"Oh," I said, puzzled. "Sure. What about?"

The woman on the other end of the phone seemed surprised. "About the bakery, of course."

I had no idea what was going on. "What about the bakery?" I started to panic. Was it on fire? Did someone rob the place and shoot everyone dead? Were we headline news and I didn't know it?

"I'm doing a piece on successful women in business. Your bakery seems to be all the rage these days and we'd love to interview you. Is tomorrow good for you? We can have a crew there around eleven."

Wow! The news wants to interview me? This didn't seem real. "Tomorrow's fine," I said, trying not to sound too excited.

"Great," Roberta said. "See you then."

Before she could hang up the phone I shouted, "Oh, Roberta?"

"Yes."

"What should I wear?"

CB   CB   CB

The camera crew was there at eleven o'clock sharp. Roberta showed up fifteen minutes later. I'd seen her on television a thousand times before but she looked so different in person. She was shorter than I'd imagined she was sitting behind the news desk. Her makeup was severe, but I guess when you're on TV, you have wear a lot so you don't look pale or dead. She was trimmed in a peach colored dress suit with peach colored pumps—and she had what we native Texans call "Texas hair." It was cut in a bob and ratted so it poofed up on top. She was very businesslike—not too friendly—not too bitchy. But as soon as the camera turned on, boy did she turn it on. She was bubbly and sweet and super Southern sounding. As soon as the cameraman let her know he wasn't taping any longer, she morphed back into what I figured to be her real self—not so bubbly and sweet—and definitely not from around here. My guess was that she was from somewhere in the Midwest—not that there's anything wrong with that.

The piece focused on me and how I'd made strides in empowering women-run businesses. It was funny because I wasn't doing it for women. I was doing it because I loved it—it had nothing to do with being a woman. I never saw it as being an issue. It wasn't something I could help anyway, right? I mean you don't get to choose whether you're a man or a woman, so what's the point? But Roberta Collins had a point. And I think it had something to do with women being able to do anything men can do—or something like that. I was just glad to get the publicity—and I didn't even have to pay for it. She went on to interview Lucy (who gave out her cell phone number to "all you single boys who like to party"—I was mortified) and Ben. He was really impressive—and smooth. He practically had Roberta eating out of his hand. She was blushing like a school girl. I couldn't help but laugh. Anyway, after all was said and done, our little bakery was featured on the six o'clock and ten o'clock news. I couldn't have been more proud. I just wished I had Henry to share it with.

Chapter 10

The school year was winding down, which couldn't have come at a better time. The cookbook had hit bookstores and the publisher agreed to spend ten thousand dollars on publicity—meaning a book tour. My plan was to coordinate the dates with the kids' summer schedule so that they could travel with me. This would leave Ben in charge of the bakery, Lucy managing the online orders and my dad to take care of my mother all by himself. I had mixed emotions about leaving. I was excited to go to places like Charlotte, Savannah, Austin and San Diego, but it was stressful thinking about putting other people in charge and trusting that things would be handled the way I would do them.

Ben assured me that the bakery would be fine without me. In my heart, I knew he was right. He was pretty much in charge anyway. But I liked to think he needed me. Lucy's current beau, the sous chef from Alejandro's, had just dumped her for the sous chef at Daniel's, so she promised me she would throw herself into her work—depressed or not. This worried me, although Lucy without a boyfriend is more reliable than Lucy *with* a boyfriend. Either way, she'd find some other shmuck to date before the ink dried on her breakup with the sous chef, so there was no sense in my getting too worked up about it. What could I say?—that was Lucy. But after my speech about how important all of this was to me and her nodding in agreement, I secretly mouthed to Ben, who was busy taking inventory, "Watch her." He smiled and gave me the thumbs up sign. *Thank God for Ben* has become my daily prayer.

The day before the kids and I were scheduled to leave for our first stop, I went to visit my mother. It was a good day. My dad was there and he was getting ready to take her for a walk. I kissed her cheek and she smiled at me and said, "Hello Claire."

"Hey Mama," I said as I wiped my lip gloss off her cheek.

She looked out the window. "Isn't it a gorgeous day?"

I followed her gaze. It was. The sun was shining—there wasn't a cloud in the sky. There was a slight breeze and the weather man said to expect warm temperatures for the next few days. I almost hated to leave town.

"Your dad's going to take me outside," Mom said as she turned to face me.

My dad took a cardigan out of the closet and helped my mother into it.

"That's nice, Mama."

"You coming with us?"

"No, ma'am. I have to go. The kids and I are leaving town for a few weeks. We're taking your cookbook on tour. Isn't that exciting?"

"That's nice, Claire."

My mother seemed to disconnect a little bit. Or maybe she didn't understand what I was saying. Maybe she forgot that she shared her stories and her recipes with me. I felt a little deflated by her reaction but then quickly scolded myself for it. She couldn't help it. She was ill.

My dad walked her toward the door and they left me standing in the room next to the window. My mother stopped, turned towards me and said, "I'm proud of you Claire."

CB CB CB

Chase, Allie and I left for Savannah. The plane took off on time and I had two hours to sit and think about the next few weeks. What an adventure. The kids were happy to be able to go with me and I was grateful for the company. I looked at my itinerary. I was scheduled for an appearance at Books A Million and a place called Kitchens on the Square (which from what I was told was a lot like Williams-Sonoma). I had no idea what to expect at the bookstore. I'd never done anything like this before. I think I was just supposed to sit at a table and sign copies and talk to people. But, at the other place, I was going to bake one of the recipes from the cookbook and pass out samples—easy enough. I felt most comfortable doing that. Butterflies flooded my stomach when the pilot came over the speaker and asked the flight attendants to prepare to land. It was show time.

The next day flew by. We left our hotel early that morning and I made my two appearances. The bookstore appearance wasn't as scary as I thought it would be. There was a decent turnout—most people browsed through the book and then came to the table where I was sitting. No one had ever heard of me—I mean it wasn't like they were lined up to see me. But everyone who did stop by and purchase a cookbook was super friendly. It was a great experience. The appearance at the cooking store went even better. Chase and Allie were excited because they got to be my assistants. They were a huge success. We made our famous chocolate chess tartlets and sold forty something cookbooks. It was a great day—and we were exhausted.

When we finally got back to the hotel, we ordered room service. The kids took their showers and were asleep by eight-thirty. I dialed Ben's cell phone to check in. He answered on the first ring. We talked about the day's events and he assured me that everything was OK—better than OK. I was relieved. Then we went from talking about the store to his latest dating fiasco (the girl chugged four beers in thirty minutes and burped the alphabet for him) and then about everything else. When we finally got off the phone I looked at the clock—it was almost midnight. Had we been on the phone together for nearly three hours?

I stretched, changed into my pajamas and crawled into the other full-sized bed. I pulled the blanket up to my chin and thought about Henry. It had been two months since he walked out of the hospital room. I hadn't heard from or seen him since then. I missed him terribly—it wasn't supposed to end that way—or at all. My thoughts drifted from him to Bryan. Talk about things not turning out the way you planned. When we got married, we agreed that if either one of us died, the other one would never remarry. Well, now I could see how that would be an almost impossible promise to keep. I've learned that the heart is supposed to love. Without love, you are nothing but an empty shell. With love, there's always hope. And I hoped to love again.

CB CB CB

After two weeks of traveling to six cities, we finally landed back at DFW. I've never been so glad to be home. The kids seemed happy, too. I couldn't wait to get back to work. I'd missed the store. I'd missed everyone that works there. I'd missed Lucy and my mom and my dad. Although, while we were away, I stayed up to speed on how everyone was doing. Mom had some tough days, where she spent most of them sleeping in her bed. Dad stayed busy collecting my mail, helping out at the bakery and running back and forth to the nursing home. Lucy kept the online ordering service afloat and had recently started dating the FedEx delivery guy who picks up our orders every day. I was worried about how this might affect our service once she got tired of him and blew him off. I secretly hoped he wouldn't take it out on my business when that happened. Really, I hoped this one lasted—for purely selfish reasons, of course.

I wasted no time in getting back to my routine. Ana still came in the mornings—and with school being out for summer vacation stayed busy entertaining the children—I jogged my usual route, and then would go to work. It was still amazing how the business had grown since this time last year. And it had been because of everyone's efforts. I could honestly say I was really beginning to feel happy again.

Today when I arrived at work, Lucy came running to me holding the newspaper. She was out of breath and clearly excited about something. I didn't know it at the time, but I definitely wasn't ready for what I was about to see.

"Look at this," she said, slapping the paper in my hands. I looked at the headline: *When Old Money Marries—A Fairy Tale Wedding.* I then saw the photo accompanying the story. My heart fell to the ground and smashed into a million pieces. It was a picture of Henry and some woman named Rebecca O'Donnell—and they were engaged. I handed the paper back to Lucy and ran to the back. I covered my face with my hands and began to cry. How could this be happening? How could he marry someone else? I don't know what I was thinking. I thought he would eventually call me, forgive me, love me—anything but this. But now it was clear that wasn't going to happen. He'd met someone else and fallen in love and was going to marry her. And I wanted to die. I felt someone behind me. It was Lucy. I looked up at her through my tears and asked, "What is it? What do you want?" I was upset with her for showing me the story. Why did she think I would want to see it? What was the matter with her? "I'm sorry Claire. I didn't know you would be this upset or I would have never shown it to you." She looked truly stunned by my reaction.

I sniffed and then said, "I'm not over him. I thought he would come back...someday. I thought...oh, I don't know what I thought. But I didn't think he would find someone else so quickly. How long could he have known this girl, huh?"

Lucy shrugged her shoulders. She looked like she was afraid to say anything else.

"I mean, who meets a girl and asks her to marry him three months later?"

Lucy cleared her throat. "Only a fucking psychopath, that's who."

I nodded in agreement and wiped my eyes. I did my best to compose myself. I took a deep breath. "I'm fine. I'm actually glad you showed me that. Now I can get on with my life." I did my best impression of a smile.

Lucy seemed relieved to be let off the hook.

I went to the bathroom, splashed cold water on my face and reapplied lip gloss. I didn't want to think about this anymore. I had a business to run.

Chapter 11

I spent the next few days going from bouts of rage to feelings of sadness to numbness and then back to rage. I still couldn't believe it. Henry was engaged to someone else and it had happened so fast. It made me question everything I thought I knew about him and our time together. I was so confused. I couldn't think clearly. I had a hard time concentrating. At work, everyone kind of stayed away from me. I would be mixing batter and then break down in tears and run out the back door. After a few minutes, I would come back into the kitchen and try and act like nothing happened. Ben made most of the decisions, although they did their best to make me feel like I was in control. Clearly, I was not.

A week after reading about Henry in the paper, I decided enough was enough. My being depressed or upset about it wasn't going to change it. Besides, did I really want to be with someone who could jump in and out of a relationship as if it was nothing? My brain hurt. I'd had all I could take.

Shauna Glenn

I left the bakery early. I phoned Ana and let her know I would be picking up the children myself. After stopping at the schools and gathering them up, the three of us headed to the ice cream parlor. We have a really neat one in town. It's like an old fashioned soda shop where you sit at the bar and order banana splits and milkshakes—except there are three video games standing in the corner, which takes a little of the authenticity out of it. Not to mention the girl working in there after school has a nose ring and hot pink hair. But they do have a jukebox that plays old music (mostly Elvis and Patsy Cline) and a disco ball that hangs from the ceiling. It really is quite charming.

Once inside, Chase and Allie ran to the counter and hopped on the swiveling bar stools. Then they proceeded to do their usual thing—spin around and around until they get so dizzy they almost fall off. I set my handbag on the counter and stopped their chairs. They giggled and the sound of their laughs made me smile. The girl with the hot pink hair approached us and we placed our orders: one hot fudge sundae with extra whipped cream and two cherries (no nuts), one banana split without the strawberry ice cream (double chocolate, add caramel sauce) and one diet coke with extra ice.

They asked for quarters—Chase wanted to play a video game and Allie wanted to pick a song on the jukebox. She can't read (being only four years old and all) but has memorized that J9 is *All Shook Up* by Elvis Presley. She absolutely loves that song and plays it every time we come here. A few minutes later, our treats arrive and we sit and enjoy them while listening to Allie's song selection. It was amazing how taking time out from feeling sorry for me really improved my mood. After another ten minutes, the ice cream had been devoured. Allie handed me one of her cherries and I took it, popped it in my mouth and bit into the juicy, sweet fruit. Are maraschino cherries considered a fruit? There's no way, right? They taste too good to be good for you.

On the way home, the kids were settled in the backseat, quietly looking out the windows. I thought for a minute about bringing up something that had been on my mind. I saw an opening and decided to go for it.

"Chase, Allie, there's something we need to talk about." I looked at them through the rearview mirror.

Chase turned his attention from the window to me. "What is it?" His face was serious now.

I wondered what was wrong, but then remembered the last time I told them we needed to talk it was to tell them their dad was dying.

I said, "oh, it's nothing bad, sweetie," as I pulled the car over to the curb and parked. I turned around and saw his face. He looked really worried.

"Are you sure, Mom? Because you picked us up from school and took us to get ice cream. You did that once before, remember? You and Daddy did that."

I hadn't remembered that part, but he was exactly right. Why hadn't I remembered that?

I reached my hand back and placed it on his knee and squeezed. I smiled and looked from him to Allie. She was watching the two of us, not saying a word.

"Everything's fine. I promise. This can wait. It's no big deal."

I turned around again, put the car in 'drive' and pulled back out onto the street. I had intended on telling them I thought it was time to get rid of Bryan's things. We needed to. I didn't think it was healthy for them for us to have all his things in the closet like he still lived there. I think we had all been secretly hoping that he'd come back one day and I had sort of been the ringleader in that illusion. But talking about it with them could wait. Maybe they weren't ready. Maybe I wasn't ready.

83

Chase asked, "What happened with Henry? Why doesn't he come over anymore? Is he mad at you?"

Wow. I hadn't prepared myself for questions about Henry, but that was dumb of me. He had become a regular at the house and now he wasn't. What was I thinking? Of course they'd wonder what happened to him. They liked Henry—a lot. They'd both seemed happy that he was in our lives. But I was so worried about how it made me feel to lose Henry that I hadn't even considered what it would do to the kids. I was sure I was the worst mother on the planet.

"Henry and I are still friends. He's just really busy and you know how busy Mommy is these days, so it hasn't been a good time for us to get together." I lied to my kids. I'd never lied to them before. So besides being the worst mother, I was now the biggest jerk on the planet. But it was all I could think to say. I mean I couldn't tell them the truth.

"Oh," Chase said. "I thought it was maybe because he's getting married to someone else."

My heart did a nose dive into my stomach. "Where'd you hear that?" I was shocked.

"From Mary Catherine at school. Her mom's the one marrying him."

I thought I was going to be sick. Of course! That's where I'd heard the name Rebecca O'Donnell before. Rumor is she was married to the son of the owner of the Houston Texans football team, divorced him, and received a substantial settlement (millions, I heard) in exchange for walking away without trying to get more. She and her daughter moved from Houston and settled here right before school started. She apparently threw a fit about putting her precious little girl in public school, but had missed the deadline for getting into any of the private schools—even after she offered to make a "donation." I also heard she tried using her connections with her ex-husband's family, but they wouldn't help her. So she "settled" on the school where Chase goes. I kind of felt sorry for the little girl. I'd seen her at school a couple of times, but had never met her mother. From the sounds of it, Rebecca was a piece of work.

As I pulled into the driveway of our house, I wondered how Henry got mixed up with her. Did she love him or did she see dollar signs? Did he really love her? We got out of the car and Ana came from inside the house and ran toward me. She told me that my dad had been trying to get a hold of me but I wasn't answering my cell phone. I reached into my bag, pulled it out and saw that my phone was on vibrate. I looked at the screen—I had fifteen missed calls—all from Dad and Lucy. This couldn't be good.

Ana took the kids inside while I frantically dialed my dad's number. He answered on the first ring.

"What is it? Is it Mom?"

"You'd better come quickly, Claire." My dad's voice sounded grave.

"I'm on my way," I said, but don't think he heard me. I think he'd already hung up.

I stuck my head in the door and said to Ana, "Can you stay? I have to go…"

She cut me off saying, "Go, go. I'll stay as long as you need me. Now go, hurry. We'll be OK."

My hands were shaking as I put the keys in the ignition and backed out of the driveway. What had happened? Was my mother dying? Had she already? Was I too late?

I drove as fast as I could to the nursing home and parked the car. I ran inside and down the left hallway reserved for Alzheimer's patients. Before I could reach room 9A, one of my mother's nurses, Joyce, met me in the hallway and told me how sorry she was and how much she loved my mother. We hugged and I felt tears well up in my eyes. That's when

I knew it. My mother had died. I stopped at the door and saw Dad, Lucy, and the doctor standing over my mother's bed. She lay perfectly still, her hair fanned out around her pillow, her face pale, her eyes closed. I hurried to the bedside and kissed her on the forehead. She was still warm. I looked at their faces. Lucy's was tear stained, her eyes bloodshot red. My dad looked the saddest I've ever seen him, and older—much, much older. My mother's illness had taken its toll on him. He was clearly exhausted. The doctor had my mother's chart and was scribbling something inside. My dad was the first to speak.

"Mary, you are the love of my life, the mother of my children, the best friend I ever had." His voiced cracked as he reached for her hand.

I started to cry. This was it. This was my mother's last day. This was the day I'd dreaded. I'd hoped it wouldn't come, but knew that it would before I was ready. I wasn't ready. It was too soon. I hadn't said all I wanted to say to her.

My dad stepped back and Lucy moved closer to her. She picked up her lifeless hand and held it close to her. She was really crying now. All she said was, "Bye-bye Mommy. I love you." She looked like such a little girl. She looked nothing of her thirty-three years. It was more like she was that twelve year old with pigtails. I ached in my heart for Lucy. She had been the baby—my mother's pride and joy—my mother's little clone. It was amazing how much they looked alike. I'm not sure I'd ever noticed that before. But standing here right now, she was like looking at a younger version of my mother.

My dad put his arm around Lucy and she buried her head in his shoulder. I could tell he was trying his best to be strong for the both of us, but what he probably wanted to do was scream out about how unfair this was. Maybe that would come later—when he was alone.

I looked at my mother's face again. She seemed so peaceful. I touched her hair and said to her, "Thank you, Mama, for being such a great mother to me. You helped me through every stage of my life. You taught me how to love, the importance of working hard to get what you want and to never give up—even when I've wanted to. But most importantly, you showed us what it means to be a family. I'm eternally grateful and I will miss you terribly." Tears streamed down my face. Lucy pulled a tissue from box on the bedside and handed it to me. I wiped my eyes and blew my nose. The sound it made was so loud that Lucy started laughing. That made me start laughing and then I snorted. This made all of us start laughing even harder. I looked over at the doctor who was watching us. He had a funny look on his face. He probably was wondering what was wrong with the three of us. I stopped and said, "We shouldn't be laughing at a time like this."

My dad chimed in, "Your mother wouldn't have it any other way."

And he was right. She would be horrified if she knew we were standing over her death bed, blubbering like babies.

The doctor asked my dad "is there anything else before we finish?"

He shook his head.

The doctor looked at his watch and said, "Time of death, 5:04." Then he noted it in my mother's chart, gave his condolences, and left the room.

Chapter 12

It was a beautiful day. The sun was shining brightly, the birds were singing their usual tunes and the humidity was low which made the August heat almost bearable. I rounded the corner and headed up the last hill toward home and thought about my mother. I wondered if there was a heaven. And if there was, was she already there? Was she with Bryan? Would they be together now—both of them healed from what took them from us? I liked to think they were, although I've never been a big believer in heaven. Heaven has always seemed like a delusional state we live in, a fictional place with all-you-can-eat-buffets and rainbows and kittens. I've always thought people believed in heaven because they hoped that there *was* something on the other side of death. The not knowing what happens when you die can be a lot to take in if you give it too much thought. So, up to this point, I haven't given it much thought. But now, having people I love so dearly gone from me, I choose to believe that there is a heaven and that Bryan was able to find my mother when she got there.

I hurried in the house and showered and changed. Ana came today, even though it was Saturday, to help me get the kids ready. The memorial service was planned for eleven o'clock that morning, with a reception to follow at Heaping Spoonful. Ben hung a sign on the window, stating we were closed for a private party. He and Maria had been preparing all morning—food and desserts and a huge variety of wines. It meant a lot to me.

I tried going to work the day before, but the minute Ben saw me, he shooed me back out the door and refused to let me come in. So instead, I drove around for awhile until I somehow ended up in the movie theater parking lot. I purchased a ticket and the biggest tub of popcorn and made my way into the darkened theater. I hadn't gone to the movies by myself since I was in college. I couldn't even remember the last time I'd seen a movie—and then it hit me. It was with Henry.

We pulled up to the church and I found my way to the family room. My mother had requested cremation, with her ashes being spread over the Grand Canyon (her favorite place in America) so there was no body to view—just an urn that looked very similar to a vase I saw in the Horchow catalog. That was fine with me. I would have been worried the whole time about how my kids felt, seeing their grandmother lying in a casket. My dad was there, all dressed up. He looked handsome in his black suit, but his face looked tired. He did his best to smile when he saw me and the children. Chase and Allie ran to him and he bent down and hugged and kissed them both. Lucy came a few minutes later, with the FedEx guy in tow (although thankfully he wasn't wearing his uniform). I shot her a look. She mouthed, "What?" back at me. I shook my head, figuring, what was the use?

People started arriving, many of them I'd never seen before. We shook a lot of hands, were given lots of hugs and encouraging words, and listened to stories about my mother. After awhile, the minister asked my dad if he was ready to begin the service. We all took our seats in the sanctuary and the music began to play. I sat next to Lucy, and Chase and Allie sat on the other side of me. My dad sat next to them. After the song was finished, the minister led the congregation in a prayer. I took the moment to look around at the crowd. There were hundreds of people there. More than sixty years worth of friends, relatives and co-workers had gathered to say "good-bye" to my mother. I felt very at peace for the first time in awhile. As I was about to turn back around to face the minister again, the door opened. When I saw Henry walk through it and find a seat on the back row, I nearly fainted. I elbowed Lucy in the side and whispered, "You'll never guess who just came in the door."

"Henry," she said, matter-of-factly.

I was stunned. "How did you know?" I tried to keep my voice down. The minister was reading some passage from the Bible.

She looked at me and said, "Because he came in the store yesterday looking for you, but you weren't there."

I had been at the movies.

"Henry came to the bakery? What for?" I was both intrigued and irritated. Wasn't he engaged?

"To check on you. He'd read Mom's obituary in the newspaper and wanted to see how you were." Lucy was clearly over this conversation because she turned her attention to the FedEx guy.

I, on the other hand, was just getting started.

"What did he say *exactly*?" My whisper was now not a whisper but more like a yell.

My dad leaned forward and Lucy saw him and tapped me, saying, "Dad's looking at us." I turned towards him and he gave me a look and put his finger up over his mouth. He shushed me. I was suddenly twelve years old again and being scolded in church. OK, maybe it wasn't the most appropriate place to have this conversation with Lucy, but I had to know what Henry said.

I turned around again and caught a glimpse of Henry. He looked in my direction and for the first time in months, we made eye contact. My heart sank, my knees weakened. Clearly, I was not over him. He smiled at me and I tried to smile back without looking too goofy, or too happy. We were at a funeral, for Christ's sake—my mother's funeral. What would she think if she knew I was flirting at her own funeral?

But what was Henry doing there? Was he just paying his respects or was it something else? Did he want to speak to me? Suddenly, I couldn't wait for this whole thing to be over with. I took in a few deep breaths and tried to focus on what the minister was saying. Toward the end, a few people stood at the podium and said really nice things about my mom. We laughed and we cried. At one point I looked down at my dad and saw him smiling. The minister closed the service with one more prayer and then invited everyone to Heaping Spoonful. Maybe Henry would show up there.

As the crowd gathered on the front lawn of the church, I made my way through the hoards of people, trying to catch Henry. I didn't know what I was going to say if I saw him, but I would think of something. I looked all around—he was no where to be found. My dad came toward me and said, "It's time to go, Claire. The children are waiting in the car." I looked around one more time and didn't see him. Defeated, I followed my dad to the car.

Once we got to Heaping Spoonful, I was still hopeful that Henry might show up and want to see me. In the meantime, I made small talk with some of my mom and dad's friends, passed out cookies and muffins, and anxiously waited for him to walk through the front door. Three hours later, everyone was gone except Dad, Lucy, Lucy's boyfriend (FedEx guy has a name—Chuck), the kids, Ben and me. It was late afternoon now and we were exhausted. I took off my high heels and poured a glass of wine. Dad and Lucy were sitting at a table and I joined them. Chase and Allie had found markers and paper in my desk drawer and were now lying on the floor, coloring.

Ben started cleaning up and I told him not to worry about it. He seemed to be ignoring me because he went about picking up plates and napkins, and wiping down tables. I would have insisted we wait until tomorrow to clean up but I didn't have the energy to stop him. Besides, I thought, "If he wants to clean up this mess then let him." Lucy and Chuck decided to leave. She kissed Dad and then me, and patted both kids on the top of the head. They barely acknowledged her. Chuck shook hands with my dad and waved goodbye to me. And then they were gone.

My dad got up and poured himself the rest of the Merlot that was in the bottle. He tossed the bottle in the trash can and looked over at me.

"Well," he said as he walked back toward the table, "I guess it's time we *both* got on with our lives."

Chapter 13

The truck pulled up and the three of us stood at the window in the front room watching as the two men got out and headed toward the front door. I picked up Allie and put her on my hip and patted Chase on the head, running my fingers through his sandy blonde hair. The doorbell rang and it seemed like we all stopped breathing. Chase and I looked at each other and I smiled at him. He said, "I'll get the door," and he headed towards the foyer.

Once inside the house, I pointed to the bedroom where the boxes and bags were waiting. The men went first and Chase, Allie and I followed behind. It had been hard, packing up all of Bryan's things, but my dad was right—it was time to move on.

I had wanted to talk with the children about going through his stuff for some time now, but the timing hadn't been right—or at least that's what I kept telling myself. It was actually Chase, the new man in our house, who suggested we give his clothes to someone who needed them. We were sitting at the table last Saturday (a week after my mother's memorial service), having grilled cheese sandwiches, when Chase brought it up.

"Mom," he said, very stoically.

"Yes, babe?"

"I think it's time we talk about cleaning out Dad's stuff."

I got a lump in my throat and was suddenly unable to speak.

Luckily for me, I didn't have to. He continued, "Dad's not coming back. We've waited long enough." He looked over at Allie who was pulling the crust off her sandwich. "Allie and I talked about it and we're OK—giving it all away."

Allie then stopped playing with her sandwich and turned to face me. "It's OK, Mommy."

I got tears in my eyes and swallowed hard. I hardly thought I deserved such great kids. "Wow." I finally said. "That must have been a hard decision for the two of you to make."

Chase shook his head and said, "No, not really. Now that Grandma Mary is with him I'm not so sad for Daddy anymore. They have each other now."

Allie nodded in agreement.

Tears streamed down my face and I couldn't believe I hadn't given these kids the credit they deserved. Sometimes it was hard remembering who the adult was.

"OK," I said, barely able to get the words to come out of my mouth. "Let's do it. Let's each pick three of our favorite things of Daddy's and give the rest of it away."

Their eyes lit up and they looked at each other and then got up from the table and sprinted down the hall to our bedroom, with Chase yelling, "I get Dad's Texas sweatshirt!" and Allie whining, "Hey, that's not fair."

I smiled as I got up and cleared the plates. I put everything in the sink and then went to the garage to get the four large boxes I'd been storing for this very moment. I made my way to the bedroom closet and began helping the kids go through and pack up their dad's things.

Now, watching the men carry the boxes from the bedroom to the truck made the whole experience real for us. None of us said anything, we just watched as the last box was loaded. We walked outside with the men and stood on our front lawn. The driver filled out a receipt and handed it to me, saying, "Thanks for the donation. Have a nice day."

I nodded and tried to smile. I took the piece of paper from him, folded it up and put it in my back pocket. We stood there in silence as they drove away. The day had finally arrived—Bryan was officially gone.

I walked into the empty closet. It seemed so big now. I'd complained to Bryan so many times about not having enough space for all my things. Well, I had enough space now. The problem was, I didn't want it. I wanted to be cramped again. I wanted to run out of room for my shoes, my handbags, my dresses. I wanted it to be too crowded to move around in—I missed the claustrophobic feeling I used to get in here. My heart began to ache and I could have very easily slipped into the state of depression I'd become comfortable in. But I wasn't going to do it. I'd made strides—we'd all made strides. I shook my head, trying to make the sadness go away. I turned, flipped off the light and closed the door on my way out. I went to the TV room where Chase and Allie were watching Spiderman 3 and I clapped my hands together and said, "All right, turn off the TV. We're going out!"

They both jumped up. Chase picked up the remote and hit the 'off' switch. Allie slipped on her shoes and they hurriedly followed me out the door. There would be no feeling sorry for ourselves today.

CB   CB   CB

School started a few weeks later and Allie was now in kindergarten. She'd turned five right after our trip to Disneyworld. Now she and Chase were going to the same school, which made it so much easier on Ana and me. I pulled up to the school and kissed them goodbye. Allie turned and waved as she ran up the sidewalk to catch up with Chase. He took her hand and I watched as they disappeared around the corner. I pulled away and headed to the bakery.

Once there, I took no time in getting right to work. We were and had been so busy for a long time now, but were used to the chaos. We all moved in an easy rhythm, each of us knowing our individual roles in making this machine work. Ben was the real key in the bakery's success—I couldn't deny it. Without him, I would have been a complete mess. I really valued his opinion and followed his leadership.

Lucy came in more chipper than usual. She was humming some song. What song was it? I recognized it but couldn't put my finger on what it was. Anyway, she seemed to sashay across the kitchen, smiling the whole time. What was she up to now?

"Hey, Claire-y Berry."

Oh my God. She hasn't called me that since we were kids. Something was definitely up. I hoped it wasn't going to affect the store in any way.

"Good morning, Lucy," I said as I grabbed an apron and threw it at her. "You're in a good mood today."

Lucy giggled. "I am. It's because I'm happy—and in love."

Oh God. "So you and Chuck are really serious?"

Lucy's smile suddenly turned sour. "Ooh, no. We're not going out anymore. We haven't for weeks."

Well this was news to me. Damn it! I'd hoped it would last—her and Chuck. I really needed my deliveries on time. It's been my experience that you don't want to piss off the FedEx guy.

"What? What happened to Chuck?" Think Claire, quick! Damage control.

Lucy waved me off. "It just wasn't working out. I was the only one giving in the relationship—if you know what I mean." She raised an eyebrow and emphasized the "if you know what I mean" part.

I was totally ooged out. How do I have these conversations with my little sister anyway? She makes everything sound like dialogue from a cheesy porno.

I let out a huge sigh and placed my hands on my hips. She was still smiling that goofy smile at me.

I rolled my eyes and said, "Well, I hope you ended it as nicely as possible as to not affect our working relationship with him."

"Relax," she soothed, "I made them think he was the one breaking up with me. It's cool. I set him up with this girl from my yoga class." Then she whispered, "She's extra bendy," and then winked at me.

I made a face and turned to walk away. I yelled out in her direction, "How do we have the same parents?"

She laughed and said, "We're more alike than you think."

God help me.

And then I stopped, spun around and walked back toward her. "Wait a minute. You said you were in love. Who are you in love with?"

"Henry," she said, and my knees went weak upon hearing his name.

"What are you talking about?" I yelled. Was she talking about my Henry?

"Oh my God, Claire, calm down. I was only joking. You're so uptight! You need to relax."

"Stop telling me to relax..." and then I stopped mid sentence. I wasn't going to let her get to me. I didn't need to relax. I was perfectly fine. She was just trying to get under my skin and I wasn't falling for it. I took a deep breath. "So, who's the new guy?"

Lucy's eyes lit up. Before she could tell me, Ben walked up and handed us each a bowl of cookie dough. "If the two of you are going to stand there and gab, you could at least make yourselves useful. We're trying to run a business here."

"Sorry, Ben," I said. Wait. Isn't this *my* business?

We stood at the counter, pulled on gloves and began rolling dough between our hands and placing it on cookie sheets.

Lucy turned to me and continued without missing a beat. "OK, so you know the day we had Mom's memorial service?"

I nodded.

"Well, we left the church and I couldn't find my sunglasses. The last place I remembered seeing them was on the church pew. So after we left here, Chuck dropped me off at my apartment and I drove back to the church to see if I could find them. I mean, it's not like they were expensive or anything, but I found them at this cute little trendy store in San Antonio and…"

"Lucy," I interrupted. "Skip that part—you're getting off subject."

"Oh, yeah," she said. "So anyway, I went back to the church and they weren't there anymore. I started walking toward the office when I heard someone behind me ask, "May I help you?"

I turned around and didn't recognize the guy but noticed how hot he was. I told him about my glasses, blah, blah, blah, and he showed me the lost and found box and there they were. We ended up talking for hours. He's new. He's single. He's my age. And his name is Father Tim.

I looked up at the ceiling and shook my head. "Please tell me that 'Father' is his first name and 'Tim' is his last."

Lucy laughed and bumped me with her hip. "No, dummy, he's a priest."

"You know you'll go to hell for dating a priest."

"Oh, give me a break, Claire." Lucy finished her bowl of dough and took the cookie sheet off the counter and walked it over to the oven, put it in and set the timer. I looked at my bowl. I'd only rolled four cookies.

She came over to me with another bowl of dough and began rolling again.

She finally said, "He's not that kind of priest. He's Episcopalian, you dope. They can date."

"I know Lucy. It's just that you..."

"I what? I like to have sex? So what? Maybe this is different. Sex isn't everything."

Who was this girl and what had she done with my irresponsible, promiscuous sister? "Oh, so you've changed over night? You're no longer into having sex?"

"We're abstaining."

When she said that I couldn't help but bust out laughing. This was *so* going to be a train wreck.

"Stop laughing," she yelled. "Be happy for me, Claire. I'm serious about this guy. It's been the best month of my life. He's really good to me. And I haven't told you about him for this very reason. But Dad really likes him."

"Wait. Dad's met him?" I asked. He hadn't mentioned anything about it to me.

"Yes, we've had dinner together twice now and he and Tim had a lot of things in common. And I asked Dad not to say anything to you because I didn't want you to get all judgmental like you are being now."

"Wow." I was stunned. I stared at Lucy. She did seem happy. And she had acted a little more maturely lately. She'd come to work on time every day and she stopped smelling of incense.

I leaned in to her and took a whiff.

She pulled back from me and gave me a weird look. "What are you doing?"

"Nothing, just seeing what you smell like."

Lucy picked up her second cookie sheet and walked toward the oven, saying over her shoulder, "Drew was right about you—you *do* have big problems."

Chapter 14

A few days after hearing about Father Tim for the first time, I decided to invite everyone over to my house for dinner. Lucy was hesitant at first, which made me think that there really was something to this relationship. She reluctantly accepted the invitation. She'd been kind of standoffish ever since the day she told me about him. I felt bad about it—in a way. Though most of this shit she brings on herself. When I mentioned Lucy's new boyfriend to my Dad, he echoed what she'd said about him, telling me what a nice guy he was. I felt so left out. I wanted to be a part of Lucy's happiness. Just because I doubted it would last (history a pretty good indicator of that) didn't mean I didn't want to be around for the show. So as a gesture of good will (and overwhelming curiosity) I phoned Lucy and Dad and offered up a steak dinner a la Claire.

At six, my dad showed up and Chase and Allie pounced on him. They played while I finished the last of the details. I opened a bottle of wine and then stopped and thought, "Wait—do Episcopalian priests drink?" I wasn't sure of the protocol so I put the bottle on the counter behind a bag of chips and decided to wait and see if anyone else brought it up. It was there if we needed it.

Around seven, the front door opened and I heard Lucy giggling. I rolled my eyes and then turned on my biggest smile and went to greet them. To my surprise, along with Lucy and Father Tim was Ben. I cocked my head to the side and said, "Ben, it's good to see you. I wasn't…" and then Lucy jumped in, "You weren't expecting us until seven-thirty, right?"

What was she talking about? She made a face that was familiar to me. It said, "Go along with what I'm saying or I will kill you." I'd seen this face a million times when she was a teenager and trying to give my parents a snow job.

"Right, seven thirty."

Ben handed me a bottle of Chardonnay and said, "Thanks for inviting me."

Oh, I got it now. This was a set up. I took the bottle from him and said, "You're so welcome. I'm glad you could come."

I would deal with my idiot sister later. Now I had to be charming in front of her new boyfriend so that I wouldn't be cast out of the loop again.

I extended my hand to him and said, "So nice to meet you, Father Tim."

He shook it and smiled, saying, "Please, call me Father."

I stopped shaking his hand and looked at him, and then at Lucy who was grinning like a teenage girl."

I didn't know what to say. He was still holding my hand.

"I'm just kidding," he quipped. "Call me Tim."

"Oh my God," I laughed, pulling my hand away, "That was funny."

"Isn't he a riot?" Lucy asked me as the four of us made our way to the kitchen.

"Hilarious." Then I pulled her aside and said in her ear, "You're so dead."

And then she said it—the word I hate hearing the most. "Relax."

Dinner turned out to be a most enjoyable event. Lucy and Dad were right—Tim was a nice guy—and smart—and funny (we'd already witnessed that, right?) and seemed to be quite taken with Lucy. The two of them looked really happy together and, for the first time ever, Lucy acted her age. I could see how Tim was a positive influence on her. It was good to see her finally growing up. Dad had everyone laughing as he told stories about Lucy and I as kids. I'd forgotten some of the shenanigans we'd pulled in our teens, but thanks to my dad and his razor-sharp memory, everyone at the table (including my children) knew all the hairy details of my childhood. It didn't matter. It felt good to sit here and see everyone having a good time. My dad's face had softened—he didn't look as haggard as he had toward the end of my mother's illness. Chase and Allie were doing well and handling the loss of their father and their grandmother very well. Ben was a hit as well. He told stories in the exaggerated way that I'd gotten used to—the kind where if your mouth is full of wine—might come spewing out your nose if you're not careful. That may or may not have happened to me. Several times during dinner I caught Ben staring at me from across the table. When I would make eye contact with him, he'd look away. I didn't know how I felt about that. We were friends. I liked him as a friend. I was a little uncomfortable about the idea that this was supposed to be some sort of set up. I don't know what Lucy was thinking. Ben worked for me. I couldn't be as successful without him. But we were just friends. Even with that hanging over my head a little, the evening was a success.

As Lucy cleared the plates, my dad made coffee and I took the coconut-crème pie out of the fridge and began slicing it. Chase and

Allie opted for a bowl of ice cream and took it to the TV room so they could watch a movie.

We had coffee and pie and talked a little while longer, then my dad looked at his watch and said it was getting late for him. I looked at the clock on the stove—it was 9:30. It didn't seem that late. We'd been having so much fun together that the time flew by. A few minutes later, everyone else was making their way to the door. We all shared hugs and Ben surprised me by kissing me on the cheek. Then he whispered, "Bye, Claire."

A tiny shiver went up my spine. I closed the door behind them and stood there for a moment, thinking about the way Ben's lips felt on my face. Then I shook my head, trying to get the image to disappear out of my mind. After all, we were just friends, right?

CB CB CB

The next time I saw Ben it was a little awkward—not for him, but for me. He smiled at me when I came into the shop on Monday and I waved to him. He came over and we went over the schedule for the upcoming week. Then he reminded me that he was going to be off for a few days. I hadn't remembered that.

"Where are you going?" I asked. I hadn't meant to sound so territorial but it totally came out that way.

"Remember, I'm going to Las Vegas for my brother's bachelor party?"

"Right." Now it was all coming back to me. Gambling. Strippers. Drunk parties. Debauchery.

I began to focus on his mouth. I'd never noticed how pretty his lips were before—they're plump, but not Angelina Jolie plump, and were the nicest shade of red. Then I remembered the kiss—which meant nothing—but had still managed to make me a little squirrelly.

"Claire? Is everything OK?"

I snapped out of my coma and realized he'd been talking to me and I hadn't responded. "What?"

He smiled. "You sort of zoned out on me for a minute."

"Sorry," I stumbled. "I've just got a lot on my mind. What were you saying?"

"I said," you should be fine because everyone else is going to pick up the slack while I'm gone."

"Oh yeah," I said as I waved him off. "We'll be fine. Have fun in Las Vegas—Sin City." And I held up my hands and made air quotes when I said "Sin City."

"OK. Well, I'd better get back to work. There's a lot to do before I go."

"Yeah, good idea," I said as I walked toward my desk. What I really wanted to say was, "don't go," but was grateful that I had refrained from saying something so ridiculous. I had to get a hold of myself—and fast.

Chapter 15

The door chimed and I headed to the front. I walked through the swinging door and there was a woman I hadn't seen before, standing at the counter, flipping through the cookbook. She was tall, with long red hair and striking features. Her clothes were designer and her jewelry—expensive. She was the kind of woman that made you feel insecure. You definitely wouldn't want to show up at a party with her—if you wanted anyone to notice you in the slightest. From first glance I guessed that she didn't have many friends. I could've been wrong, but I doubted it.

I smoothed my hair back and tied my apron a little tighter. She saw me and smiled. I immediately hated her.

I plastered on a smile and said, "Hello. Can I help you?"

She was flipping through a book of photographs when she turned her attention to me.

"Yes, you can. I need to order my wedding cake and everyone in town (and she emphasized 'everyone') said I *must* order my cake from this place."

"Great," I said, reaching for an order form and a pen. "Do you have a particular cake in mind?"

The red headed woman flipped back to a page she'd marked and said, "I like this one, but would need five tiers instead of three. My fiancé is inviting practically the entire city of Dallas." She waved her arms around when she said this.

"OK." I began making notes on the paper. "What flavor would you like?"

"White chocolate, with raspberry filling. And I would like the raspberries to be organic."

"OK, not a problem," I said as I continued to write.

Then she continued, "My fiancé, Henry, doesn't like eating fruit that isn't organic."

The name stung the deepest part of my soul and I thought I might vomit.

I looked up at her and must have turned pale because she asked, "Are you all right?"

I nodded and said, "Yes, it's just a little warm in here. So, your fiancé's name is Henry?

"Yes, Henry Sugarman. Do you know him?" She was grinning from ear to ear. I suddenly had the urge to stab her with my ink pen.

"I know of him. I know the family." I lied.

She leaned in a little closer to me and said, "I guess everyone knows who the Sugarmans are."

"So your name is?" Like I didn't already know.

"Rebecca O'Donnell. O-D-O-N-N-E-L-L"

I copied everything down just exactly as she said it (as if I were an idiot) and she went on and on about their stupid wedding plans.

"When's the date?" I asked. How was I going to be able to do this? I couldn't make Henry and Bridezilla's wedding cake, could I?

"December first," she seemed delighted in saying. "Isn't that divine? A Christmas wedding."

"Yeah, it's magical." I tried not to sound too sarcastic, but wasn't sure she would have picked up on it anyway. She was too into herself and her precious wedding talk to notice that I was scowling uncontrollably.

I tried to act normal. And I was curious about something. If I wanted information I was going to have to pull it together. "How did you two meet?—if you don't mind me asking."

"Oh, it's the best story," she cooed.

I wanted to throw up right there—all over her dumb clothes and ugly shoes (the shoes were actually amazing, but I would never give her the satisfaction of knowing that I loved them).

"Tell me," I said, trying to sound sincere.

"Well, Henry and I went to the same university (I could name it before she said it), SMU, and he pledged a fraternity and I pledged a sorority and our clubs had a lot of functions together. So we met freshman year and became really good friends—but never dated. He was shy and I had a serious boyfriend who went to another school, but we hung out together a lot. After college I moved to Houston and he stayed here. We sort of lost touch for twenty or so years. But when I moved back here a few months ago, I looked him up and he'd just ended a relationship, so it was perfect timing. And we just sort of picked up where we left off."

It made me sick to know that the "relationship" she was talking about was me. I had a giant lump in my throat—it was getting hard to breathe. I tried to contain myself long enough to finish the order and see her out the door before breaking down in the middle of the bakery on a busy Tuesday afternoon.

The next few minutes were a blur to me. I remember sitting on the floor, crying. Someone in the bakery must have told everyone in the back that something was wrong with the crazy lady because I looked up and Ben, Lucy, Maria and Celia were standing over me. Lucy bent down and helped me get up. Ben ran and got a glass of water and brought it to me. There was a small crowd gathered and I tried to smile—to assure them that I was OK—although it was clear I was not. Lucy walked me back to the kitchen and had me sit at my desk. Maria and Celia took over the front and Ben and Lucy watched me—like maybe something might happen.

Lucy was the first to speak. "What happened? Are you OK?"

I looked at her and then at Ben. "I'm fine. Just had a little break down is all."

Lucy asked, "What upset you? I haven't seen you like this since…" and then she stopped.

I knew what she was going to say. There was no need to go on. I guess she realized that too.

Ben said, "So you're all right then?—because I'm leaving now. And I won't be back until Monday."

I could tell by the way he said it that he didn't think I could handle it. I was beginning to believe that, too—for more reasons than the obvious.

Chapter 16

I started spending more time with my dad. He came over just about every night at dinnertime. Sometimes we went out to eat, and other times we took turns cooking. I guess you could basically say we were a couple—a couple of sad sacks. The kids loved his company and I had to admit it was nice having another adult around—even if it was my dad. We talked about a lot stuff—life in general—more specifically, me and the bakery and Lucy and of course, Mom. Dad and I recently went through the attic in his house (which took up almost an entire week!) and cleaned it out. The kids and I had a huge yard sale on his front lawn, selling old clothes, worthless framed art that my mother was forever buying at those starving artists sales (there was a reason they were starving), and yes, someone even bought my mother's collection of Southern Living magazines. I asked the woman what she was going to use them for and she said, "The recipes, of course." Hmm, why hadn't I thought of that?

By the end of the two-day sale, we raked in close to a thousand dollars. I couldn't believe we made so much money. Dad decided to save it for a road trip for all of us to go on over spring break to the Grand Canyon. His plan was to rent an RV and drive the one thousand, eighty-two miles all in one day. Chase and Allie were excited about the trip and began asking me every day how much longer until spring break. I was already sick of hearing about it, so I posted a calendar on the refrigerator so they could flip page after page and find the month of March. Chase finally realized that getting from October to March would take awhile and explained to Allie that they were better off getting excited about Christmas. I suggested a much quicker payoff—Halloween. That was even better, they said, so then they started driving me crazy, planning their costumes. I, personally, was dreading the holidays. It would be our first without my mother and our second year without Bryan. I tried not to think about it. I actually had a lot of things to be happy about—but I was having a difficult time remembering what they were exactly.

Lucy and Father Tim—or just Tim, however, knew exactly what they were happy about. It was getting really serious. They spent every waking moment together—but still no sex, Lucy informed me. She was even going to church. They had been coming over to my house on Sundays for lunch and Lucy was relentless, trying to get me to join them for Sunday service. I hadn't taken her up on it yet. God and I weren't exactly on the same page these days. I'd been pretty mad at him (or her) for the last few years now and didn't see myself getting over it anytime soon. I guess it was safe to say I was holding a grudge. Dad had been going, and had taken the children with him several times, while I've stayed home and made lunch for everyone. Maybe I would go one day. I just wasn't ready yet.

Lucy had changed drastically—that was obvious. Not her personality; she was still the same goofy sister she'd been all her life, but something had changed. She seemed more grounded, more responsible, more sure of herself. I was able to rely on her a lot more at the bakery. I didn't have to ask Ben to keep on an eye on her anymore. I could spend more time focusing on the cookbook. I'd been traveling around Texas a few days a week, promoting and signing cookbooks, meeting people, giving demonstrations and sharing baking tips. I was really getting into the whole experience and, along the way, I was learning a lot about myself. I never thought I would enjoy doing something like this, but it turned out, I was. To date, we had sold more than 100,000 copies of the cookbook and the publisher had already reprinted twice. I think it was doing better than anyone anticipated—and the online ordering had surpassed our in-store sales. I was grateful to be so busy. It gave me much less time to feel sorry for myself.

At night, when I lay in bed, I became extremely lonely. I thought about Bryan, but the image of him wasn't as clear. I couldn't smell him anymore, his scent no longer on the pillows, in the closet or on my clothes. I had to concentrate really hard to remember the little imperfections on his skin—the mole on his left shoulder, the scar on his shin (was the right one or the left one?—the picture in my head was fading). One night I fought with myself for half an hour trying to remember which leg his scar was on. I jumped out of the bed and went to the TV room where I kept the photo boxes. I found the one labeled 'Panama Beach' and lifted the cover and furiously flipped through picture after picture until I found one that showed Bryan and Chase sitting on the beach, digging in the sand. There it was, on his right shin. I let out a sigh and repeated several times, "mole on his left shoulder, scar on his right shin, mole on his left shoulder, scar on his right shin." I placed the photo in the box and placed the box back on the shelf. I walked down the dark, quiet hallway back to my room.

Some nights I didn't think of Bryan at all—it was Henry who consumed my mind. My heart ached for him still, even though I knew it was over. He was getting married and I was baking his fucking wedding cake. How's that for irony? Was there any question now that the universe hated me? Only a few times did I consider putting Ex-lax in the cake batter, and then imagined all the guests running to the restroom at once, with Rebecca crying out that her wedding had been ruined. I couldn't help but smile at the image of her black mascara running down her overly rouged cheeks as she stood there sobbing in her ivory dress. Henry wouldn't be able to console her because he, too, would be in the bathroom battling a serious case of diarrhea. I laughed out loud at the image for a second and then the laughing turned to crying—uncontrollable crying. I had to figure out a way (a healthy way if possible) to get over him. My attempts so far had been futile. Someone knocked on my door just then and I sat up in bed and said, "Come in."

I wiped my eyes on the sleeve of my t-shirt and saw Chase standing next to the bed.

"Are you OK, Mom?" He looked very concerned.

I sniffed, "Yes, honey, I'm fine. I just get a little sad sometimes."

"Do you want me to lay down with you until you fall asleep?"

I smiled and pulled the covers back. "Would you mind?"

Chase crawled in the bed with me and we lay there, looking at each other in the dark.

"I miss Daddy, too," Chase finally said.

"I know, sweetie." I was doing my best not to start crying again.

He continued, "But I also miss Henry." His saying this surprised me and took my breath away.

"You do?"

"Yeah. I thought he might move in with us and you wouldn't be sad anymore."

116

Well, so much for not crying again. As I boo-hooed, Chase reached across me and got a tissue off the night stand. He handed it to me and I wiped my eyes and blew my nose.

"We're going to be just fine, baby. OK? Don't worry about me. You're too young to have to worry about grown-up stuff." I grabbed another tissue.

Chase looked at me very seriously. "But I'm the man of the house now. Dad said for me to take care of you and Allie."

I stopped wiping my eyes and looked at him. "He did?"

Chase nodded.

"But you weren't even six yet, when Daddy died. How do you remember what he told you?"

"You don't forget something like that, Mom."

I smiled, patted his cheek and watched as he drifted off to sleep. How had I gotten so lucky to have this sweet little man in my life, looking out for me? Maybe God wasn't so bad after all. He had done something right.

CB   CB   CB

I dropped off the kids at school and headed to work. I'd just walked in the door when I heard the front bell. I yelled, "I'll get it," and hurried through the swinging door. I stopped dead in my tracks when I saw who it was. Henry looked at me and smiled, awkwardly.

I couldn't move—I didn't know what to say.

"Hello, Claire. How are you?"

I was still speechless. I couldn't will my body to move, my brain to function, or my mouth to speak. It was getting uncomfortable—well, more uncomfortable than it already was.

Finally I managed to say, "Henry."

I moved closer to him, but stayed behind the counter. We stood there for a minute, neither of us speaking.

Henry broke the awkward silence by asking, "Is there any way we could go get coffee?"

I pointed to the coffee maker—"There's coffee right here."

"Right," he said. "Somewhere that's not here?"

I couldn't read him. I couldn't figure out exactly what he wanted. What was he doing here? Why did he keep showing up in my life when he'd made it perfectly clear he didn't want to be part of it?

Still, my heart wanted to be near him. "Sure. Let me get my bag."

I went to the back, ran into the bathroom, leaned over the sink and splashed water on my face. I looked in the mirror and told myself, "Pull it together." When I came out, Ben looked at me funny and I said, "I'll be back in a little while."

He asked, "Is everything OK?"

"I don't know," I yelled as I left the kitchen.

Butterflies were swimming in my stomach. I tried not to look nervous, but was doing a shitty job of it. My hands were shaking uncontrollably. Henry held the door for me and we crossed the street, neither of us saying a word. I pointed to Shot O'Java and he nodded. We entered the coffee shop and he asked what I wanted to drink. I shook my head no and said, "Nothing—I'm fine."

I found a table and watched Henry as he ordered a latte with two Equals. He was more handsome than ever. I guess being engaged will do that to a person. I tried to distract myself from thinking about him by looking around the room at the other people. It was pretty deserted. There was one man furiously typing on his laptop and an older woman sitting in the corner, reading a book. Just then, Henry sat down and the familiar smell of him suddenly overwhelmed me. I took a deep breath and looked at his face. He smiled nervously at me and I suddenly wanted to cry. I had to fight really hard not to. As weird as this should have felt, it didn't. It was comfortable—even though neither of us said anything for a minute.

Henry took a sip of his coffee and said, "You look great."

"Thanks," I said, trying to smile. "Is that why you wanted to talk?—to tell me I look great?"

"No. I was just trying to break the ice." Henry looked down at his coffee cup.

"Well, consider the ice broken," I said as I touched his hand with mine. I pulled it away as soon as I did it. I hadn't meant to—it just happened.

He looked at me and said, "I wanted to tell you that I had no idea Rebecca—my, my..."

"Fiancé," I interrupted.

"Right, my fiancé, was going to ask you to do the wedding cake. If I'd known I wouldn't have let her do it. I wouldn't do that to you. I would never hurt you on purpose. She doesn't know about us—I mean she doesn't know that the relationship I was in before her was with you. You don't have to do it, Claire."

Suddenly, I felt hot. No longer did I want to jump his bones—now I wanted to kick his ass. This was what he wanted to talk to me about—his fiancé? I'd heard enough. I stood up, pushed the chair under the table and said, "You don't have to worry—it's OK. You can let your conscience off the hook. Besides—it's what I do for a living." I left him sitting there as I walked toward the door. As I reached for it I stopped, turned around, and said (rather loudly), "And for the record—I would never hurt you on purpose either." I didn't wait for him to respond. I pushed the door open and headed back out into the street, my legs so shaky I was afraid they would fail me. The next sound I heard was a car blaring its horn at me as I ran out in front of it, almost getting hit. A part of me wished it could've been that simple—just run over me and get it over with.

Chapter 17

I hadn't seen Henry since that day in the coffee shop. I had, however, seen Rebecca on two occasions. Once she came in the bakery to finalize the wedding cake from hell. And then I ran into her another time at the French café on the edge of the square. I was there picking up lunch for Lucy and me when I heard someone behind me saying, "Yoo-hoo, Heaping Spoonful lady." I turned around wondering what kind of weirdo yells out something like that in the middle of a crowded restaurant. Then when I saw her smiling her big toothy grin at me, obviously oblivious to everyone else in the place, it became crystal clear—this kind of weirdo. She motioned for me to come to her table, where she was sitting with three other women who looked frighteningly just like her. Ugh. Why me? I cursed under my breath and did my best to smile as I made my way to her table.

She apologized while still smiling, "I'm sorry, darling. I have forgotten your name."

I suddenly noticed how big her teeth actually were—they were *way* too big for a human mouth, but perfect for a horse. I wondered if she had equine somewhere in her family tree.

"Claire." I said, while still staring at her gigantic teeth-filled mouth.

"Oh, that's right, Claire. I'm so sorry. I must have wedding mania on the brain."

I smiled through gritted teeth. "How terrible for you."

"Thank you," she said, without really listening to me. She was too busy going around the table, introducing me to her friends—who were also her bridesmaids. Then she said, "Everyone, this is the person who is making my wedding cake." And the words "wedding cake" came out a few octaves higher. She couldn't seem to be able to contain her excitement. She clapped and giggled and the rest of them joined in. Wasn't she a little old to be getting this worked up about a wedding? I mean, she'd been married before—at least once that I knew of. What was all the giggling and the squealing about? I had to get out of there. I listened to her go on a few minutes more about her ultra-fabulous wedding and when she stopped to take a breath I took the moment as an opportunity to get the hell out of there.

I said, "I really must be going—I've got people waiting on me to get back with lunch." I held up the to-go bag to prove what I was saying was true.

"All right, then. See you on December first!" she said, practically singing.

I tried not to vomit as I exited the restaurant. I made a decision then and there that one of us had to move. I couldn't keep running into the two of them. It was causing me too much stress. I hurried back to the bakery and told Lucy about my encounter as the two of us sat and ate our sandwiches. Her eyes got bigger and bigger as she listened to me recount what had happened. She also agreed with me that they should move somewhere else. Then she shook her head and said, "I don't know why you're doing this to yourself."

I put my sandwich down and swallowed the bite I had in my mouth. "Doing what to myself?"

"Why you're making their wedding cake? It's bizarre. Why don't you just call her and tell her you can't do it?"

Lucy was suddenly getting on my nerves. "Because..." And then I paused. Why was I doing this to myself?

"Because why?" she asked. "You think because maybe it lets you stay close to Henry? This way you're connected in a kind of sick, unhealthy way that keeps you from moving on with your life? I mean, what are you going to do after the wedding is over?—bake the cake for her baby shower?—or their anniversary parties?"

Lucy struck a nerve. I felt my face get hot and I picked up my sandwich and threw it in the trash can. I started to walk away when she grabbed my arm and said, "Claire, I'm worried about you. We're all worried about you."

That was it!

I looked across the room and saw Ben staring at me out of the corner of his eye. Had he been listening to our whole conversation? Was he worried about me too?

I turned back to Lucy and snapped, "Look, little sister, I appreciate that you're concerned, but, really, do I need to get advice from a girl, who until recently, thought that a long term relationship was anything over two weeks? Or from a girl whose idea of having something in common with someone meant getting matching tattoos? Because I really don't think you're qualified to be telling other people how to live their lives, thank you very much."

I left her standing there, grabbed my purse and walked out the back door. I got in my car and drove home. Ana was in the kitchen, unloading the dishwasher. I put my keys and my bag on the table and walked toward my room without saying anything. I shut my bedroom door, lay across my bed and cried myself to sleep.

I felt a tapping on my shoulder. I opened my eyes and saw Allie sitting next to me on the bed. "Are you sick?" she asked. What time was it? Had I been asleep all afternoon?

I rolled over and smoothed her bangs out of her face. "No, I was just tired."

Allie jumped up and down on the bed and yelled, "Good—cause it's Halloween and we want to go trick-or-treating when it gets dark!"

Right, it was Halloween. I stood up, stretched, and thought back on the day. I had seen my share of ghouls and goblins already. I laughed to myself, thinking about Rebecca and wondering which she was—a ghoul or a goblin? As I went in the bathroom to freshen up, I remembered the terrible things I'd said to Lucy. Oh, she probably hated me. I was so mean to her and all she was trying to do was help me. I left my room and went to the kitchen. Ana was getting ready to leave. We said goodbye and I watched her get in her car and drive away. I checked on Chase and Allie—he was writing his spelling words in alphabetical order and she was trying on her costume. She insisted on being Hannah Montana even though I tried telling her that the night would probably be filled with dozens of other girls dressed up as Hannah Montana also. She said she didn't care—so I didn't care.

I picked up the phone and dialed Lucy's number. She answered and we both said, "I'm so sorry," at the same time. I laughed and she said, "Jinx, you owe me a Coke."

I felt relieved. "If I buy you a Coke will you forgive me?"

She replied, "There's nothing to forgive—it's not like you didn't say anything that wasn't true."

"I know," I said. "But I didn't have to be mean. I was just angry and I took it out on you. It didn't have anything to do with you. I'm sorry, Luc."

"It's OK. But I have just one question."

"What's that?" I asked.

"What time are we trick-or-treating?"

I guess some things never change.

Chapter 18

The house was filled with a wonderful, sweet aroma. The turkey was done and sitting on the stove, waiting to be carved. The weather had turned uncharacteristically cold for this time of year—the weatherman saying there was chance we might get snow. My dad was busy bringing in the wood that he'd picked up at the store and was getting ready to start a fire. Chase and Allie were taking turns running down the hallway, sliding on the hardwood floors in their socked feet. Thanksgiving had been our favorite holiday in the past. But it didn't feel the same to me this year. Dad and I exchanged smiles as we passed each other in the kitchen. He needed matches. I took some out of the drawer and handed them to him, asking, "You OK today?"

He nodded and said, "You gotta take what life gives you Claire. It's better than the alternative."

Was it? I thought. I remembered the last Thanksgiving we'd had together—all of us—before Bryan got sick. It was held at my parents' house—my mother always cooked the turkey. I was in charge of the potatoes, the salad and, of course, dessert. Lucy couldn't be relied on to actually show up for dinner, so we gave her the menial task of bringing the rolls. Mother always kept extra in the pantry in case Lucy was a no-show. If she did come (and remembered to bring the rolls) our mother would hide the back-up ones so Lucy wouldn't get her feelings hurt. I always thought that was unnecessary—let Lucy know she wasn't dependable, I'd say—but Mother always said to me, "You can't do that to your child, Claire—it's cruel."

I never understood that until now. My mother had been right. You have to give people a chance if you want them to succeed. Boy, did I have a lot to learn.

There was nothing special about our last Thanksgiving together as a family. Had I known it would never be the same after that day, I would've tried to make better memories. I did remember something about it—Bryan was tired and looked tired. He'd put in a long week at work. After we ate my mother suggested he lie down and take a nap— he'd earned it, she said. While we were cleaning up, he went to my old room and slept for the next three hours. I had to wake him when it was time to leave. He said he felt better and that was it. Neither one of us thought anything more about it. But now, looking back, I guess he was already sick. We just didn't know it.

The door opened and Lucy yelled, "Happy Thanksgiving!" I ran to the front door to greet them. Chase and Allie came running into the room and took a bowl and a dish from Tim. Yes, my sister actually helped prepare food. I wasn't sure how it would taste, but she definitely got an A for effort. Tim and I hugged and he commented on the weather. I helped them out of their coats and we all headed to the family room, where Dad had just finished building the most spectacular fire. We stood there admiring it while Lucy went to the kitchen and opened a bottle of wine. She brought back four glasses, handed one to each of us and then poured the cabernet. We were about to toast when Chase said, "I want to toast."

Allie chimed in, "Me too."

I put my glass down, went to fetch two more wine glasses, filled them with sweet tea, and then handed one to each of the children.

"Now we're ready," I said. The kids looked happy to be included.

We went around the room, each of us telling what we were thankful for. I started. I said I was thankful for my kids and my sister and my dad. Chase said he was thankful that school was out for a week. Allie said she was thankful that Christmas was coming. By the way, these were the same things they were thankful for going on two years now—so there was no real surprise when they said it. Dad said he was thankful for his health and for his family. Lucy turned to Tim and told him she was thankful that he'd come into her life and saved her. She got tears in her eyes when she said this. It was really touching, seeing Lucy so happy. Tim smiled at Lucy and then turned to me and asked, "Would you mind holding my glass for a minute?"

Surprised I said, "Sure," as I took it from him. Then Tim reached into his pants pocket and pulled out a box. I looked at Dad, who gave me a funny look and flashed a smile (he knew about this!), and then back at Tim. He got down on one knee and opened the box. Lucy gasped. I gasped. Inside the box was a beautiful princess cut diamond solitaire ring. Lucy covered her mouth with her hands and Allie said, "Wow!"

Wow was right!

Tim's voice cracked as he said, "Lucy, will you marry me?"

She started jumping up and down and screaming, "Yes, yes, yes!"

Lucy held out her hand (which was now shaking) and Tim took the ring (his hands were shaking, too) from the black velvet box and placed it on her finger. He stood up and the two of them kissed.

The rest of us stood there, staring at them, utterly speechless. My sister was engaged. This was definitely turning out to be a memorable Thanksgiving, and we hadn't even eaten yet. We took turns hugging and kissing and admiring her ring. Dad and Tim shook hands and then my dad embraced him and jokingly said, "This is my baby—you know that, right? You better take good care of her so she doesn't try to come live with me."

Tim laughed nervously. He was probably glad that was over with. I must say I was impressed that he proposed to Lucy in front of all of us. What a brave man. Lucy danced across the room, practically floating on air. It was so great to see her like this. She deserved to be happy.

After a few more minutes of celebrating, we finally sat down for dinner. There was so much excitement in the room. Lucy talked a hundred miles an hour—already coming up with ideas for her perfect wedding. The rest of us sat there, eating and listening to her ramble on for the next hour. You would think the girl was on speed—my brain hurt just listening to her. By the time dessert was served, she had already decided on a date—February 14th—how original—and the colors—hot pink and steel gray—and the honeymoon—Hawaii. Poor Tim. All the man could do was sit there and nod like an obedient husband to be. He definitely had his work cut out for him.

Chapter 19

I woke up to the sound of thunder clapping ferociously in the sky. I got up and walked to the window and smiled. The view was something out of a movie or what you would see on the Discovery channel. The conditions seemed treacherous—like a hurricane was going to hit any minute—although, to my knowledge, there had never been a hurricane in this part of Texas before. The trees were being whipped about by warp-speed winds, the rain drops the size of golf balls. And I couldn't be happier. The storm had been an answer to my prayers. It was a day I had been dreading for a while now, but Mother Nature seemed to be taking pity on me and gave me an early Christmas present.

The wedding cake from hell (as it had been lovingly dubbed) was almost done and waiting for the finishing touches. Rebecca O'Donnell had only made nine changes to it from its original design, and it was nearly time for it to finally make its debut. Even I had to admit it was spectacular. But that was more a compliment to me—I mean I'm the one who created the masterpiece, for Christ's sake. She only got credit for being smart enough to get me to make the Goddamn thing in the first place.

As I put on my clothes and then grabbed my raincoat from the hall closet, I thought about Rebecca and how upset she must be about the weather. Storms like this keep people inside—nobody wants to get out of the house on a day like this—not even to go to a wedding. Dad came in just as I was getting my keys and I pointed to the TV room. "They're watching a movie."

"OK," he said, making a beeline to the coffee maker. "Stay out of trouble," he added as I opened the door and headed out into the rain.

I drove slowly. The rain was coming down so hard that it was difficult to see the road in front of me. There were hardly any cars out. Again, I smiled. As I made my way to the square, I began humming the song, *going to the chapel and we're gonna get married,* but I changed some of the words to, *going to the chapel and we're gonna get soaking wet…gee he really loves you in your soggy wedding dress.* I laughed to myself and then I thought, *there might really be something wrong with me.*

I pulled into the parking lot and thought again about Rebecca and how she was probably standing in front of the window, cursing the storm. She might have even felt like her day was ruined. And then I thought about Henry and how handsome he would look in a tuxedo. I wondered if I'd see him when I went to drop off the cake. Part of me hoped not, but there was this other curious side that wanted to see him any chance I got.

I stepped out of the car and ran through puddles of water to get to the door. I jiggled the key as the rain pounded on top of my head. I finally managed to get the door unlocked and went inside. No one was there yet. The bakery wouldn't be open for another hour. I hung up my wet coat and went in the bathroom and towel dried my hair. I looked in the mirror—I looked just like a wet dog. After pulling my hair back into a ponytail, I opened the cooler door, propped it open and walked inside and carefully picked up the cake. As I went to exit the cooler, something happened and the door shut, locking me inside. I screamed and put the cake back on the shelf, careful not to let it topple. I pushed on the door, kicked it, and yelled for help. None of these things worked. I was stuck in there. I looked at my watch. I needed to have the cake at the country club in exactly two hours. I began to panic. It wasn't finished. I needed at least an hour, maybe more, to finish putting on the last of the fondant, the flowers and the beads. I looked at my watch again. If I was lucky, Ben would get to the bakery early and I could make up some time.

It was cold. I was freezing. I started to shiver. I tried pacing back and forth to keep warm, but it wasn't working. I checked my watch over and over, thinking somehow that might make the time go by faster. It didn't—time seemed to be standing still. Finally, I heard something. I walked to the door and banged on it. "Help! Help!" I screamed. There was a voice on the other side of the door—I couldn't tell who it was. I heard someone messing with the door and then it opened. It was Ben. Thank God. He looked at me, obviously shocked to find me in the freezer. Without hesitating, he took off his sweatshirt and handed it to me. "Thank you," I said, my teeth chattering so badly I could hardly speak. And then, out of nowhere, I reached my arms around his neck and kissed him on the mouth. We held it there for a minute and then he started kissing me back. Then I pulled away from him, startled by my actions. He opened his eyes and stared at me, neither one of us saying anything. The moment became excruciatingly awkward. I couldn't decide if I'd really wanted to do that (kiss him) or if I was just glad to be rescued from the freezer. Would I have reacted that way if Maria had been the one who had found me in there? I hardly doubted it. I didn't have time to analyze the kiss—or my actions, and I knew Ben probably had a million questions but I had no time to answer them. I was confused and I was *sure* he was confused, but we were short on time, so any discussion about it would have to wait. We'd have to come back to this later—or maybe never (which part of me was hoping). I had lost a good forty five minutes and now was in a rush to get the cake delivered on time. Ben said nothing still, but grabbed the other side of the board that held the cake, and the two of us carried it to the counter. We worked in silence—awkward silence—me on the cake—Ben on getting the store ready to open. I knew he was watching me—I could feel his eyes on me. "What is it?" I finally asked, although I knew exactly what it was.

"Nothing," he said. Then he opened his mouth again like he was going to say something about what just happened and then he stopped again. He finally asked, "How long were you locked in the cooler?"

"About an hour," I said in his direction.

"Geez."

Then he started laughing. I finished putting the last of the beads around the edge of the bottom tier and asked, "What's so funny?"

"The first time I got locked in there I had to wait for three hours before Maria found me. I scared her so badly she almost hit me with the mixing bowl. Then she cussed at me in Spanish for the next fifteen minutes before I was finally able to convince her that it wasn't a prank—I was really locked inside."

The image of that made me start laughing too. And then I said, "Wait a minute—the first time? How many times have you locked yourself inside?"

Ben held up his hand and said, "five."

CB   CB   CB

The rain had let up some, and we covered the cake and carefully loaded it into the back of the van. After we secured it, making sure it wouldn't fall Ben looked at me and said, "Why don't you let me take it?"

"Not on your life," I said as I carefully pushed the door shut.

Just then Lucy pulled up and got out of her car. "Hey," she said. "I'm going with you. I gotta see this." She pulled her hood over her head and ran toward us.

I rolled my eyes. "Fine," I said. "But there's not going to be anything to see. I'm just going to drive to the country club, find the Bluebonnet Ballroom and drop off the cake. End of story."

"Right," she said as she winked at Ben. He shook his head and turned to go back inside the store. Just then thunder roared in the distance.

"Get in before it starts pouring again!" I yelled and Lucy jumped in the front seat next to me.

We pulled up to the Riverdale Country Club with minutes to spare. I had butterflies in my stomach as I tried to imagine exactly where Henry would be at this moment. From listening to Rebecca go on and on about their wedding day, I knew the ceremony was going to be held somewhere in the country club, with the reception following in the Bluebonnet Ballroom. I parked at the front door and stepped out into the rain. We carried the cake inside and before I could ask the receptionist where we were supposed to go, she pointed to her right and said, "Sugarman wedding—that way."

Hearing that name made me feel sick to my stomach. I composed myself as best I could and Lucy asked me, "Are you OK?"

"Besides the fact that this cake weighs a ton?—Yes, I'm OK."

Lucy smiled at me, but she knew I was full of shit. Nothing about this was OK, but it certainly was about to be closure. I was going to deal with this head on and then hope and pray I wouldn't completely lose it. This was going to be the period at the end of the sentence—whether I wanted it to be or not.

We found the ballroom and it was breathtaking. Rebecca had done a beautiful job putting this together. The linens were a cream color, with gold-rimmed table ware and Baccarat crystal. There were red poinsettias and white roses everywhere. The tables were filled with ivory candles. The service people were busy lighting the candles and setting a table with champagne glasses. One lady came toward us and pointed to where the cake was to be set up. She looked at me and smiled, commenting on how beautiful the cake was, but I couldn't say anything in return. Lucy spoke for me and replied, "Thank you. My sister here is the artist."

I wasn't trying to be rude—I was just a little overwhelmed. Maybe it hadn't been such a good idea after all—me coming down here. Seeing this place—knowing what this was all about was more difficult to handle than I'd thought. I tried to focus on the cake—yes, that's what I had to do. Lucy and I carefully lifted it from the board and placed it on the table. We stepped back and admired it, making sure it was centered on the table. After a few more minutes, we left the ballroom and headed toward the front door to leave. I turned to thank the receptionist and that's when I saw Henry. He was standing no more than twenty feet from me, dressed in his tuxedo, talking to a man also wearing a tuxedo. My heart leapt in my stomach and I felt I might be sick. Henry turned and saw me—his face turning white as a ghost. I ran out of the country club, leaving Lucy behind. I jumped in the driver's seat and started the engine. Lucy opened the passenger side door a few seconds later.

"What's the matter?" Lucy said, sounding out of breath. She must not have seen Henry.

"I saw Henry and I panicked," I said.

"Oh shit! Are you all right?"

"No, I'm not." And then the tears fell. I pulled out onto the street and right in front of a car. It honked at me and had to swerve to avoid hitting me.

"Pull over and let me drive," Lucy screamed. I did as I was told. We switched places and I was crying so hard then I couldn't see. It was really happening. Henry was going to marry someone else—and I was just realizing it.

Chapter 20

Lucy pulled the van into the parking lot of Heaping Spoonful and I got out and ran inside. The kitchen was busy, everyone working to fill the orders. I ran past them without saying anything and went into the bathroom and shut the door. I put down the toilet lid and sat on it, covering my face with my hands. I heard voices on the other side—I could make out Lucy's and Ben's. She must have been filling him in on what had taken place. She had such a big mouth. There was a knock on the door. "Not now, Lucy," I said through my tears.

"It's Ben. Can I come in?"

That was worse. I tried to stop crying and sound somewhat normal. Ha!—normal. What a joke that was. "I'll be out in a minute."

The door opened. I looked up and saw Ben standing there, looking at me, his eyes very serious. He came closer and knelt down in front of me. I had no idea what to say. His doing this had really thrown me off. What was he doing?

"Claire," he started. He looked at me, then the floor, then at me again. "How long do I have sit back and watch you do this to yourself? That guy doesn't deserve you. I've tried to stay out of it, but I can't do it any longer. You deserve a man who looks at you and thinks you're the most beautiful woman in the world—someone who wakes up every morning and thanks his lucky stars that he's got you in his life—someone like me. I've wanted to tell you how I felt about you for so long, but I was afraid to. I'm not afraid anymore, Claire. I want to be with you. I want to be that guy who makes you smile again."

I was floored. I didn't know what to say. My heart stopped—I couldn't breathe—I couldn't move. I just sat there and listened as Ben told me everything I'd been waiting to hear—except not from him.

Ben reached up and pushed my hair out of my face. He pulled some toilet paper off the roll and handed it to me. I managed to wipe the tears from my face. I tried smiling at him, but it came out weird.

He was still staring at me, probably waiting for me to say something. That was a normal reaction. I mean, someone practically telling you he loves you and wants to be with you usually generates a response. Just as I was about to tell him…tell him what? Tell him thank you for saying all the right things—but hey, I don't feel the same way about you? That seemed cruel. And the last thing I wanted to do was hurt Ben.

He stood up and reached for my hand. It was so awkward. I took it and stood up and faced him. Just then Lucy came in the bathroom and said, "You're not going to believe this! Henry is out there and wants to see you."

Ben let go of my hand and walked out of the bathroom past Lucy. "Ben, wait." I said after him.

He walked outside and let the door slam. I turned to Lucy and said, "Tell Henry to hold on just a minute."

Lucy yelled, "What's going on?"

I didn't stop to answer her. I ran out the back door to find Ben.

He was there, standing against the wall, lighting a cigarette. "I didn't know you smoked," I said as I stood in front of him.

"Only on days I make a fool out of myself." He took a long drag and shoved the lighter back in his pocket.

"Ben, I don't know what to say. I mean I care about you. I really do. And those things you said in there—they were the nicest things anyone has said to me in a long time."

Ben cut me off. "It's OK, Claire. I kind of knew how it would go. I just thought I would give it a shot."

I stepped closer to Ben and leaned in, kissing him on the cheek. He smelled of tobacco, cake batter, and chocolate. "Are we OK? I don't want to lose you as my friend."

Ben laughed. "What you mean is you don't want to lose me as your manager."

I smiled at him and said, "OK, that too. But more than that, I really cherish our friendship."

He puffed the cigarette once more and blew out the smoke. He dropped it on the ground and stepped on it, putting it out. He then moved closer to me and wrapped his arms around me. I put mine around him and we stood there for a moment, neither of us saying anything. I closed my eyes and tried to imagine what it would be like if he and I were together.

He pulled away from me and said, "Go on—go see what the jerk wants."

I smiled at him, turned and walked towards the door.

"Claire." His voice sounded serious again.

I looked back at Ben. "Yes?"

"Be careful."

"I will," I said as I hurried inside to find Henry.

Back inside, I ran into Lucy, who seemed very confused. "What's going on Claire? What did Ben say to you? And why is Henry here?"

My knees felt weak. My stomach was filled with a million butterflies and all of the sudden I was experiencing moments of confusion, anger, and sheer happiness. It was a trip.

I grabbed Lucy by the shoulders and said, "I don't know, he said he wanted to be with me, and I don't know." There. I think I'd answered them in the order in which they were asked.

I left her standing there looking even more confused, and then I took a deep breath before pushing open the door to the front of the store. Henry was standing there, still in his tux, his face...I don't know. I couldn't read it yet. I couldn't tell if he was sad, confused or all of the above. He saw me and came toward me, his face softening. It was that face I'd fallen in love with. I tried to remain stoic although inside I was dying.

He stopped in front of me and I crossed my arms across my chest. "What are you doing here, Henry? You're supposed to be getting married. Did you? Get married?"

Henry shook his head and I felt a wave of relief wash over me. "No, I couldn't do it."

"I'm sorry, Henry. That must have been a tough decision for you. But that doesn't explain why you're here."

Henry's eyes welled up and I was afraid that if he started crying, I would completely lose it. "Because I'm an idiot and I wanted to tell you that. I should never have walked out on you that day in the hospital. I should have let you explain everything—although, your sister did actually."

"When?" I asked. When had Lucy spoken to Henry? "Last week. She called and asked me to meet her for coffee and I did.

She explained everything and at the time I told her it didn't matter. But when I saw you today, I knew I couldn't go through with it."

"Why?"

"Because I still love you—it's always been you. I just let my pride get in the way." Henry reached out and touched me, sending a shiver up my spine. I closed my eyes and let him fold me in his arms.

Then I quickly pulled away. "What if you hadn't seen me today? Would you have gone through with the wedding?" Suddenly this was beginning to feel less romantic and more contrived.

"Claire—it wasn't going to happen. I just couldn't figure out how to make it stop. That guy you saw me talking to? I was telling him that I was calling off the wedding. I was on my way to Rebecca's suite to tell her. She knows—everyone knows."

I felt overwhelmed. I was confused. "Knows what?"

"She knows I'm in love with you. I told her I was sorry—that I should never have gotten involved with her because my heart belonged to someone else—to you, Claire."

Suddenly I was angry. I ran out the front door and down the street in the rain. Henry came after me, yelling, "Claire, wait, please!"

I stopped and he caught up to me. I turned to face him. "Why did you do this? Why did you make me into a crazy person for all these months? We wasted so much time, Henry! And I've been so miserable. Life doesn't give us many second chances and you blew it—you blew it with your pride and your need to punish me. That was cruel, Henry. And now you're here and you think you can just waltz back into my life and we can pick up where we left off? Is that what you think?"

The rain was pouring down. We were both soaked. Henry stood there, not saying anything and then, "I'm sorry Claire—for all of those things. I was a prick. I didn't mean to hurt you. I was angry and I felt betrayed. But I know we can be great again. I love you, Claire."

Suddenly, everything was crystal clear. No longer did I feel the pain in my heart. It had vanished. And I knew then, better than any other time in my life, exactly what it was I wanted.

I smiled at Henry and he moved closer to me. I put my hand on his chest and said, "But I don't love you anymore." He stopped short, his face looked shocked by my words.

"Oh my God, Henry—I don't love you. I thought I did and you said all the right things—everything I wanted you to say, but I don't feel it anymore. I think I'm finally over you."

I was ecstatic. I felt like I could fly. Henry's power over me had disappeared. I had survived it—but not only that, I knew another thing for sure.

Henry was about to say something when I took off running back toward the store. He called out after me, but I kept going. It didn't matter what he had to say. I had to hurry back.

I opened the front door and raced inside, nearly knocking over one of my customers. "Sorry, Mrs. Biggers!" I yelled as I hurried to the kitchen. I went over to Ben and when he saw me he did a double take. I reached up, threw my arms around his neck and kissed him hard on the mouth. He put his arms around me and kissed me back, his lips softening. It was magical. Maria and Celia started giggling and Lucy shouted, "Would someone please tell me what the fuck's going on here?"

I pulled away from him and said, "OK, let's get one thing clear—you can never smoke again."

Ben smiled and kissed me on the nose. "Deal."

Chapter 21

The music started playing and Dad and I smiled at each other. Lucy took her place next to him and I kissed her cheek before heading down the aisle. Chase and Allie were standing at the front of the church looking on as I walked toward them. Chase looked very handsome in his tuxedo and Allie was a princess in her pink satin gown. As I reached the front where the priest was standing, I looked over at Tim. His forehead was beaded with sweat and I didn't think I'd ever seen someone so nervous before. He looked back at me and I smiled at him. He looked like he was ready to faint. I stood on the other side of Allie, and then and the priest motioned for the congregation to rise. The music stopped and the violinist began playing as we all watched my dad walk Lucy down the aisle. She was radiant. I was so proud of her—proud to be her sister. She had grown up so much in the last year—most of that thanks to Tim. They were an interesting couple—not generally two people you would put together. But somehow, they just worked. I looked over at Ben, who was sitting on the front row. He smiled at me and mouthed the words, "I love you." I blushed—I couldn't help it. He did that to me. It was still unbelievably amazing how crazy I was about him. He had been there all the time, right in front of my face and I never noticed. He'd been patient—he'd been supportive—he'd been the best friend to me and I almost blew it. Lucky for me he was so patient or he might have given up on me a long time ago.

Ever since that first kiss we'd become inseparable. I was the happiest I'd been in all my life. I'm not saying I wasn't this happy when Bryan was alive; it's just that it had been so long now, it was hard to remember, but I was sure I was. I mouthed "I love you," back to him and then turned my attention to Lucy.

The ceremony was beautiful and, true to form, my sister insisted she and Tim write their own vows. Tim's voice cracked as he recited his loving words to her—the sincerity poured out of him so effortlessly. Lucy cried, I cried—I even think my dad cried. The priest announced them husband and wife and Lucy shouted out, "Woo hoo!—we get to have sex now!" before locking lips with Tim.

The church went dead silent, except for Ben, who busted out laughing. I would say I'd never been this embarrassed before, but that would be a lie. One of Lucy's many gifts was embarrassing me. Both the kids looked up at me and I just shrugged my shoulders. What else could I do? I turned to Dad who had his head down, probably wishing he was anywhere but here. But really, did we expect anything else from her?

We exited the sanctuary and gathered in the lobby. Ben found us and reached down and scooped up Allie and leaned in and kissed me. Chase looked up at him just then and Ben noticed this and said, "Good job, man—give me one of these," and held out a fist. That's what men do, Lucy told me—they knock fists. Chase and Ben's relationship was getting better and better all the time. At first Chase wasn't sure he liked the idea that Ben and I were seeing each other. Chase thought

Ben was too young for me. I said, "For one thing, how do you know he's younger?—He could be older than me for all you know. But you're right—he *is* younger than me, but only by five years. Five years is nothing when you get to be my age."

Then Chase said, "But doesn't he work for you? Isn't that weird—or illegal?" I laughed out loud and patted his head. "No honey, it's not weird *or* illegal. It just is what it is."

He made a face at me and said, "That doesn't make sense, Mom."

But it made perfect sense to me.

I'd shared Chase's concerns with Ben and he understood. He was taking it slowly and trying to be friends with him without going overboard. Kids can see a snow job from a mile away—Lucy told me that also. That was another thing—I started getting advice from Lucy—now that should have been weird or illegal.

We left the church and drove to the country club. That rainy Saturday months ago when we had taken Rebecca and Henry's wedding cake over there (the wedding that never happened), Lucy decided that was where she wanted her reception. Later she'd asked me if it would be too weird for me if she had it there and I assured her that that part of my life was over. She said, "Great—because I've already booked it." I rolled my eyes.

There were only about fifty people invited to the wedding, so the humongous Bluebonnet Ballroom wasn't necessary. Instead, she chose the more intimate Magnolia Ballroom, which was more beautiful anyway, I thought. Lucy had stuck with her original color scheme, hot pink and steel gray—which turned out better than I'd imagined it would. She chose stargazer lilies and pink roses and the very non-traditional Mexican food buffet. I was in charge of the cake. Lucy wanted it to be a surprise. I crafted three tiers of what looked like wrapped gifts, stacked them on top of each other and covered them with a light gray rolled fondant, finished with hot pink ribbon and bows made out of the same fondant. The cake was a vanilla cream with raspberry and dark chocolate filling. It was the prettiest cake I'd ever made—I knew she would love it.

The reception turned out to be a blast. Everyone stuffed themselves with cheese enchiladas and beef fajitas and then hit the dance floor. Lucy had hired a local band that covered 80s and disco music. The margaritas were overflowing and went down so smoothly that after my second one I began to feel less nervous about the speech I was about to make in front of everyone. The kids got into the spirit, dancing and running around the room, and even my dad looked the happiest I'd seen him in months.

Ben seemed to be right at home. He danced with Lucy and with Allie and I sat at the table and watched and smiled. I felt like I could really breathe. I no longer felt like the universe hated me. I stopped waiting for the other shoe to fall. I took in a deep breath, closed my eyes and thought of Bryan. I felt like he would be OK with all of this. He'd want me to be happy. He'd said I would love again. For the first time since his death, I believed that.

When the music slowed down, Ben came over to where I was polishing off my third margarita and asked me to dance. I could feel the heat wash over me and my knees buckle slightly, and I didn't know if it was him that did that to me or the tequila or both. I decided it was both. He took my hand and we walked out onto the dance floor and I knew everyone was watching. I felt like a princess at the ball—and it wasn't even my party.

The End...or is it?

And then...

Chase opened the door of the RV and we all stepped out and took in the view. It was magnificent. It was amazing how small and insignificant you feel when you're standing on the edge of one of life's great wonders. This was my seventh or eighth trip to the Grand Canyon and seeing it never got old. I carried Allie and Ben held Chase's hand as we all made our way to the edge of the cliff. Dad joined us a few minutes later and we stood there, gazing upon what we all agreed was the most beautiful place in the whole canyon area. Lucy and Tim honked the horn as they pulled up alongside the RV. They had opted not to travel with us in the rented bus (being that they were still "doing it" every day and Tim was a screamer--as I was informed by my perverted sister—I was fine with them staying in motels along the way, thank you very much) so there was plenty of room for my dad, me, Ben and the kids to sleep comfortably.

Tim and Lucy got out of the car and stood next to us, none of us saying anything. The view literally took our breath away. Dad took the urn containing my mother's remains and held it up, and asked, "Everyone ready?" I took in a deep breath and nodded. Ben grabbed my hand and squeezed it. Tim put his arm around Lucy and we watched as our dad lifted the top off the urn and grabbed a handful of the ashes. He opened his hand and we watched as the dust blew out into the air. Tears filled my eyes as I thought about my mother. If I turned out to be half as great a woman as her, my kids would be the luckiest, most loved children on the planet. I definitely had big shoes to fill. Dad passed the urn and each of us took a handful and released the ashes into the wind just like he had done. We stood there a little while longer and then Allie said, "I'm hungry—when are we going to eat?"

Dad picked her up off the ground and said, "How about right now?"

She smiled and said, "I want a hot dog."

"Hot dogs it is," he said as he turned and walked towards the RV.

Final word

Rebecca O'Donnell did end up getting married—I even made the wedding cake, if you can believe that. Apparently Rebecca doesn't hold a grudge. She met an aging millionaire and accepted his proposal after only knowing him three weeks. He died later that year and left everything to his golden retriever, Ollie. Rebecca sued his estate (and the dog) and lost. She was last seen around town canoodling with Wendy Baumgartner—Dallas's richest lesbian.

Henry stayed single for awhile until meeting Jenny Summers, Miss North Texas 2006. I'm told the two of them, after a whirl wind romance, ran off and got married in Cabo. They're now expecting twins.

Lucy and Tim just celebrated their first wedding anniversary. Apparently they still have sex every day and Tim is still a screamer.

Dad sold the house and moved into an assisted living community. He's too busy to help out at the bakery anymore because he was just elected social chairman. His days and nights are filled with bingo tournaments, movie night and baking class. Guess who helps with that?

Chase and Allie are doing exceptionally well. They made it through the rough patch much better than I did. They are the people I admire most.

As for Ben and I—we're doing just fine. We got married six months ago at city hall in front of the justice of the peace. The only people in attendance were Lucy, my dad, and the kids. It was a Wednesday. Oh, and I made my own wedding cake.

I've been sick lately—but don't worry, it's nothing serious. The doctor says I should feel like myself again…in about nine months.

The End

Recipes

Banana Nut Bread

(Recipe courtesy of Paige Killian)

4 large eggs
1 (18.25 ounce) box yellow cake mix (without pudding)
1 (3.4 ounce) package of banana flavored instant pudding mix
1 cup water
¼ cup vegetable oil
3 ripe bananas, mashed
½ cup chopped walnuts
½ cup chopped pecans

Beat eggs at medium speed with an electric mixer until thick and pale.

Add cake mix, pudding mix, water, and vegetable oil, mixing well.

Stir in bananas and nuts.

Pour batter into 2 greased and floured (8.5" x 4.5" x 3") jelly roll (loaf) pans.

Bake at 350 degrees for 1 hour. Cool in pans on wire racks for 10 minutes. Remove from pans and cool completely.

Yields: 2 loaves

Fudge Pie

(Recipe courtesy of Julia Ann and Frances Glenn)

1 - 9" deep dish pie crust

1 ½ cups sugar

1 stick of butter, melted

1 ¾ ounces cocoa

1 teaspoon vanilla

½ cup evaporated milk

3 eggs

In large mixing bowl combine the sugar and cocoa, mix until well blended.

Add the butter and mix well.

Add the eggs and beat for approximately 2 ½ - 3 minutes.

Add the milk and vanilla, mix well.

Pour batter over into pie crust.

Bake at 350 degrees for 30 minutes.

Let cool on a wire rack for at least 2 hours before serving.

Garnish with fresh whipped cream and chocolate shavings, if desired.

Yields 8 slices

Shauna's Key Lime Pie*

(*not an original recipe—I just perfected it)

8 egg yolks

2 (14-ounce) cans sweetened condensed milk

7 ounces Key lime juice

1 package (12 ounces) cream cheese

6 ounces Cool Whip (or similar)

¼ cup confectioners' sugar

2 (9-inch) deep dish graham cracker pie crusts

Beat egg yolks at medium speed with an electric mixer until pale yellow.

Add condensed milk and lime juice to yolks, beating well.

Add cream cheese, cool whip and confectioner's sugar, and mix well.

Pour filling into the pie crusts. Bake at 350 degrees for 20 minutes or until outside edges are set.

Let cool on a wire rack. Chill in the refrigerator for at least 2 hours before serving.

Each pie yields 8 servings (or 4 if you live in my house).

I would be a total loser without…

Oprah…yes, it's true. I said from the beginning that if I wrote a book I would credit her for encouraging people to live their best lives. It was only after going to her seminar in Dallas that I realized I wasn't living mine.

My girlfriends…KB, Ellen, Heather, Amber, Tabitha, Sarah, Cathy, Tracie, Tamara, Melissa, Wendy, Jill, Susanne, Christi, and Allison… you all were forced to read my stuff probably more times than you wanted to. I urged you to tell me the truth about what you thought, but what I really wanted was for you to tell me how much you loved it. Thanks for always lying to me.

Jenn…my first editor—ever. You made me a much better writer. You reined me in when I needed to be and pushed me to tell it like it is—even when I knew it would come back to bite me in the ass—and it has on more than one occasion. I never would have had the guts to write what I was really thinking if it wasn't for your encouragement. You told me the truth (for which I hated you sometimes—not really) and you were always right. I'm lucky to have you as my friend.

Carrie…You laugh at all my stupid jokes and that's really why I do this—to make people laugh. Thank you for being an awesome sister-in-law—and more importantly, thanks for being my friend.

Jen…You are a talent. The book cover is everything I envisioned and more. Thank you for being able to read my mind when I was certain my mind had left the building.

Patricia…I couldn't do any of this without your help. You are the other mother to my kids, and having you in our lives makes it easy—and possible—for me to pursue my dreams. Thank you for minding the store while Mother is away.

Hal Brown and *Fort Worth Texas* magazine… I'm sure you had no idea what you were getting yourself into when you agreed to let me write a monthly column in your magazine. The day I met with you I felt like I was being sent to the principal's office. I will always remember you as the first person who gave me a shot at this writing thing. Thanks for believing in me before I ever did. Don't worry, I'll keep writing for you as long as you let me—or until the good people of Fort Worth revolt against me and you pull the plug on the whole thing. That should be any day now, right?

Mom and Julia Ann…ah, mothers. God love 'em. They're there for us our whole lives and then bam!—one day they make for great writing material. It's the ultimate compliment, no? Thanks for always being good sports and for always supporting me. Oh wait—you didn't know I was writing about YOU?

Robert Guinsler…my super agent and secret lover. You could tell I was awesome the minute you met me and I knew then that you were some sort of super special literary agent—kudos to you for knowing a good thing when you saw it. Seriously, I totally love and respect your ability to find a diamond in the rough (in case you were wondering, we are talking about me). My only regret is that I don't see you enough.

Monika…my publicist/new best friend. What can I say?—you are the coolest. Thank you for taking me on and making my complicated life less complicated. Without your guidance and masterful organizational skills, I would still be trying to find the SEND button on my keyboard. The way you talk people into liking me speaks volumes at just how persistent you really are. My condolences to your husband.

Dad…maybe my biggest fan—and possibly one of three—total. Thank you for your support and for reading every piece of crap I've ever written. I know it's hard to root for a story that you can't possibly relate to—being that you are a man and all. But still, you always give me wonderful advice—for which I always take—okay, well mostly always. But seriously, you are the first person to read anything and everything I write. And because it's important to me that you like all of it tells the story of why I desperately need therapy. I love you.

Presley, Riley, Harley, Ethan...my four awesome and inspiring children. I always knew I wanted to be a mom. And now that I have you, I'd like to rethink my position—just kidding—sort of. Seriously though, motherhood is the role I cherish the most. I think I might even be a better mom than I am writer. And even though I've never won any mother of the year awards, I know I'm a pretty good one—and that what happened was the FedEx guy got lost on his way over to deliver it to me. It should be arriving any minute now. And no, I never put Mountain Dew in any of my kids' sippy cups before—that I remember.

Tommy...the ultimate butt of all my jokes. You know there's a special place for men like you. You know what I'm talking about. The men that have to put up with loud mouth, smart ass women like me. Don't you worry, as soon as I'm dead, I'm sure you'll meet some nice, young, respectable woman with D cups and a vast knowledge of pop culture. You'll have loads in common—especially when you try and introduce her to Van Morrison and she thinks he's some friend of yours. Honey, you deserve it. I will be cheering you on from hell—because let's be honest—that's exactly where I'm going...if there is one. The good part—I'll know everyone there, so don't worry about me. You just enjoy your life with your new supermodel girlfriend and don't worry for one second that she won't like your wrinkled face, your silver hair or your old man legs. I'm sure she loves that in a mate. See, I'm trying to say thank you and it comes out like an insult. Seriously, I love you more than you'll ever know. And none of this—at all (except for the going to hell part) would be possible without you—and your unending, unconditional, undying love and friendship. XO

Short Stories

The Business at Home

I know lots of people who work from home. It's become very common place in our society and more and more people are taking advantage of working from home. Basically all some people need is a lap-top and a cell phone to be able to do their jobs. It's sort of like a "mobile" work station. I run into lots of people at places like Starbucks and they're doing just that—working. The idea is a nice one—much the way I would want to work if I held a real job. I say "real" because I don't feel I have an "official" job. Well, I didn't until recently. I write (I guess I really don't need to tell you that since you are reading what I'm writing at this very moment), and have four children. That's enough for me. Sometimes it's too much. They all suck a lot of the time and I wish I could just be alone for five minutes. But can that happen? Apparently not! And now there's another element that has been thrown into the mix.

My husband (bless his heart) sold his company a couple of years ago and since then has been "semi-retired." Actually it's been eight hundred and four days—not that I'm counting. I know this because ever since he quit working, he has been home—with me. And I say "semi-retired" because he's only forty-two. He is busy consulting with people and researching his next venture, but until then, he's home twenty-four-seven. It was nice at first, having him around. He takes the kids to school sometimes, picks up the little one from preschool and takes her for ice cream from time to time, and has been there for every "first" that our twenty-month old has had. This was the first child he has really been able to watch "grow up."

These things are nice right? Right! But here's the problem. He's driving me crazy!! Every time I turn around, there he is. One day I was busy gathering up all the towels to start a load in the washing machine and he stopped me and asked, "You got a minute? I'd like to discuss Hybrid cars versus non-Hybrid cars with you."

Oh for the love of Pete! I dropped the load of towels on the floor in front of him and smiled—because I'm nothing if not accommodating. "Sure I've got a minute—take two. But I think I can sum it up by saying Hybrid—definitely Hybrid is the way to go." There, can I get back to what I was doing?

He looked perturbed and said, "You can't just say 'Hybrid.' We need to set a meeting and discuss the pros, cons, the technical advances, the environment, etc. I'll send you a meeting time via email and I'd like you to reply and we'll meet upstairs in my office." Someone please shoot me! And you know what? He's serious. Also, he yells my name across the house—"Shauna, Shauna—come here, quick!" The first time he yelled to me I thought, "Oh my god—something's happened. He must be in some kind of danger. Maybe he's cut himself and is bleeding to death." So I ran towards the sound of his voice and found him in the kitchen—eating leftovers while standing up—and without a plate or napkin and the refrigerator door standing wide open. I was out of breath from running to see what the matter was and now I find him—alive and clearly not bleeding. The vein in my head started to throb. Not only is he not bleeding to death (which doesn't sound so bad right now), but he's dropping food by the forkful all over the freshly mopped kitchen floor. I'm sure he has no intention of cleaning it up which means one thing—I'm going to have to do it. Instead of blowing up at him I politely get him a plate to use and ask, "What is it that you needed? I assumed something was wrong since you yelled for me to 'come quick.' So, here I am. What is it?"

As he shoved more leftover spaghetti in his mouth he asked, "Did you get my email?" Okay. I was trying not to lose my temper. I quickly tried counting to ten—someone said that's supposed to relax you when you feel angry. It wasn't working. But I was going to try not to sound annoyed or angry.

"What email?" I get lots of emails from him. I bet he sends me four or five a day. Not only do I get emails, but I get these weird meeting requests from him that I either have to 'accept' or 'decline' or 'set a new time.' That's too much for me so I just always hit 'accept'—though I rarely show up for the 'meeting.' I just learned recently though that he's serious about the meetings. So now I'm trying to actually attend if I have time. It's odd to me to get an email from someone who is sitting directly across from me at the breakfast table. But I do. I also think it's odd to have to set 'meeting times' to discuss things like what plants we're going to put in our yard this spring. But we do. I got such a 'meeting request.' It read something like: March 22, 2-2:30pm, meet in office to discuss purchase of vegetation for home garden. Why do we have to have 'meetings'? Why can't we just talk, informally, over coffee? Now when I used to work in a "real" job outside the home, I would get such meeting requests, which is appropriate. But I'm not in the "corporate" world anymore. I'm at home—washing clothes! And he wants to set up formal meeting times? You've got to be kidding me!

Instead of answering me, he said, "come over here and let me show you something." I didn't know where this conversation was going, but I was busy. I was right in the middle of wrapping a birthday present. I didn't have time for this. What does he want?! Instead of screaming out loud, I did what he asked. I stood next to him and together we stared inside the refrigerator. I didn't get what we were doing. Was this some sort of Buddhist ritual? Are we praying to the refrigerator god? "Okay, it's the fridge," I said sarcastically. "In America it's what we use to store cold food in."

He snapped back, "I know that. Can you tell me what's wrong with this picture?" I surveyed the contents of the fridge—are we out of orange juice?—no. Hum, we have lunch meat, cheese, mayo, wine, and yogurt—no, doesn't look like anything is missing to me. I shook my head and asked quizzically, "no soy sauce?" My husband laughed and pulled me closer to him. Then he let me in on what was missing.

"The refrigerator is unorganized. There are no labels on any of the shelves and I can't find what I'm looking for. There's no order in here."

I swear to you there's not a jury that would convict me. Instead of bludgeoning him to death with the contents of my unorganized refrigerator I asked him, "what is it you're looking for and I'll find it for you."

He shook his head and said, "No—you're missing the point. It needs to be organized so everything is in the right place." Now he really is joking. There's a right place and a wrong place to put the pickles? He clearly needs a hobby—one that doesn't involve me organizing things.

Anyway, has he forgotten who he's married to? I am in charge around here. This is *my* kitchen and *my* messy fridge. I am the utilitarian one and I take great pride in having things unorganized. How dare he come in here and try to make things run more efficiently. He had certainly crossed the line this time.

I knew my face was red because I could feel heat washing over my entire body. I think he was a little afraid of me at this point because he said, "Never mind. We can talk about this later."

Oh no we can not! As far as I was concerned this conversation was over. But instead of saying what I really felt, I just stood there like a dope and agreed to clean out and organize the offensive refrigerator. At least now that I had caved I could get back to my very busy day! I had a nail appointment in exactly twenty minutes!

There are hundreds of stories just like these, but I don't have enough time to write them all down. You see I work now—for my husband. Since being at home, he has decided that now he's the CEO of the house.

He has hired a professional organizer to work with me and show me how to get things in "order." He's given his input on all sorts of things that I used to be in charge of. He's the CEO all right—Chief Egghead Overlord.

God love him. He's doing his best. He's used to being in charge. And now I'm the lucky girl who he gets to fetch his coffee, file his...whatever he files, and wash his underwear. Bonus! Anybody hiring? Please? I've got just the man for the job.

Coming Out of the Closet

Sssh. I'm writing this from inside the closet. Not the figurative kind, but the actual closet. This is what I have been reduced to—hiding from my eighteen month old son. I hate to admit this, but I feel I have no other choice. He follows me around the house, pulling at my legs and a lot of the time, my pants; even more often pulling them down to my knees. This is okay when we're at home, but try explaining to some stranger in public why I'm not wearing any unmentionables under my mentionables. That's only happened once. I really learned a lesson that day. It was like, note to self: wear undies under your loosely fitting workout pants.

So anyway, as I was saying, I'm in the closet. I've been in here for about ten minutes now, and he hasn't found me yet although I hear his voice. He's nearby—I think he's rummaging through the trash can in my bathroom. Maybe I should hold my breath; he's only a few feet from me—oh crap! I think I'm about to sneeze! Shoo!—false alarm. Anyway, I can hear his baby foot steps roaming through the house while his nose is trying to pick up my scent. He's calling, "mama, mama" but I'm acting like I don't hear him. I realize this is questionable parenting, but I'm sorry—I'm tired, okay? Believe me, I don't enjoy doing this. But I just want to sit here with my laptop and my bottle of wine and bag of chips and have five freakin' minutes to myself. Is that too much to ask?

I haven't even finished making dinner. I was in the kitchen cooking a pot of soup but I got flustered with all the leg pulling and whining and decided to hide for awhile. I'm not proud to admit this, but I actually said to him, "Look over there!" And when he looked in the direction I was pointing, I ran out of the room. This happens a lot during this time of the day—not the hiding (although that is becoming more frequent), but the whining and the crying. It's the witching hour (or hours) at our house. The time between five o'clock and eight o'clock (when he finally goes to bed) is pretty hectic. Well, that's putting it lightly; it's the suckiest time of my day! Every time I try to do anything other than hold him, he stands at my feet, begging me to pick him up. It sounds awful doesn't it? You may be asking, "Why don't you just pick him up? He's a baby." And to that I would say, "I have been holding him for a good part of the day." We've played with Elmo which he pronounces "but-bo" and blocks and even played outside. But at some point I have to put him down so I can get some things done. People expect to eat around here and I have yet to see anyone else make the effort. There are only so many days you can call pizza delivery.

So far, no one is on to my hiding in the closet thing. Which is odd since it is five thirty on a week night. No one else seems to care where I am right now except the baby. My husband (I'm sure) is tucked away peacefully in his office upstairs, oblivious that this even goes on in the afternoon and my two oldest daughters are in their rooms doing homework. My four year old chooses this time to watch her favorite show, The Simpsons (another example of my questionable parenting) so it's just me and the little one. Do you feel as sorry for me as I do? I didn't think so. You're probably thinking that I shouldn't have had four children if I didn't want to deal with everything that having four children includes. And I would tell you that I didn't know what I was getting into, okay!—and we didn't have a television for the longest time, so we didn't have much else to do. Relax—we have a TV now, so there will be no more babies.

Before I hid in the closet, I used to hide in the bathroom. But that didn't work for very long. At first, no one bothered me. They didn't ask what I was doing, it was kind of assumed. I think they were even grossed out a little. But what they didn't know was that I wasn't doing anything. I would take my book or the most recent People magazine in there and just sit and read. And it was heaven. Then, the little pests began questioning my going habits. And you know who the ring leader was?—my husband. He totally sold me out. I heard him say, "Mommy's not going potty; she's in there hanging out." *Traitor!* So from then on, the little devils would knock on the door and when I wouldn't answer or open, they would lie on the floor and stick their little hands underneath the door. I couldn't help but laugh, but still I remained quiet. I thought that maybe they'd get bored or distracted and move on. But that never happened. After fifteen minutes of unending questions like, "Mommy, are you in there?" or "Mommy, are you going number one or number two?" or "Mommy, are you *ever* coming out?" I eventually succumbed to the beating awaiting me and appeared from the sanctity from what was once a clever hideaway.

That's when I had to come up with another place to hide. Like I said, I'm not proud of this—it's just my reality right now. I know one of these days he's going to lose interest in me altogether, so I should enjoy all of the attention he gives me, right? I mean I'm already experiencing this with my two oldest children and even my four year old seems to have a handle on the whole independence thing. I should feel lucky that someone loves me so much and can't stand being away from me, but instead of that I feel like a total victim. This time every day I find myself feeling sorry for myself and being angry and resentful towards my husband and older children who hardly lend a hand.

Oh! Look who it is! I've been found. My son is smiling at me with his crooked grin and I suddenly feel like the worst mother on the planet. How could I hide from the most adorable little boy in the world? He is so forgiving; he probably thinks this is a game. He wraps his arms around my neck and sits in my lap, reaching his sweet little hand in the bag of chips. We sit in the dark, munching on Ruffles, totally ruining our dinner. He looks up at me and laughs, poking me in the nose, saying "mama." I squeeze him tight, kissing his cheek, which makes him squeal with laughter. After a few more minutes of Mommy and son time, we come out of the closet and I resume cooking dinner. Then all of the sudden it seems, everyone appears and pitches in and helps. Even the baby lets me put him in his high chair. The evening ends on a high note; we eat dinner and watch television together. Still, I can't help but think about tomorrow and how it will start all over again. And remember if you need me, I'll be in the closet.

Sex, Scandal, and Barnes and Noble

I'm constantly trying to come up with new ways to bond with my kids. It's hard today competing with things like Xbox, "That's So Raven", and the internet—but I persevere. One day I decided to take three of my children-- ages 13, 11, and 5, to Barnes and Noble. On the way, I explained that I wanted each of us to come up with one book that we could read together as a family. The two younger girls thought the idea was great, but my oldest was a different story. Since becoming a seventh grader her favorite line is "are you serious?" after everything I say. So after the obligatory statement (that I could have bet money on was coming and would have been right!) I willingly blocked out her obvious disdain for me and the very air that I breathe and turned up the radio, singing with fervor to the song, "you give love a bad name" by Bon Jovi. I pulled into the parking lot with the two younger ones singing along with me. My teenager sunk down in the back seat and shouted, "You all are so weird—I hope I don't see anyone I know!"

Having successfully embarrassed my oldest child (another thing I can check off my list today) we hurried inside. They scattered like...oh, I don't know, a herd of something that scatters...and I began looking through the section of new fiction, hoping to find the next great novel to enjoy once the crumb snatchers go to bed. As I was flipping through one of the books, I saw (or rather felt) my oldest child standing next to me, holding the new Carl Hiaasen book. I smiled my approval at her and she just glared back at me. I forgot—I'm not supposed to look directly at the beast known as a "teenager", for fear of being turned to stone. I quickly recoiled and decided to keep my acknowledgement short and to the point.

"Very good," I said as I took the book from her. She then asked for money for Starbucks, where I in turn automatically reached into my wallet and handed her a ten dollar bill. It's much easier doing this than causing a scene—I learned that a long time ago. This isn't my first day on the job. Anyway, what is it with this generation of kids who drink coffee?—and not just coffee, but espresso? When I was a kid, there was only Folger's and if you asked for some, you were told "no" because it stunted your growth. End of story.

The second child to appear was my five year old, who was being supervised by the middle child. These days, I don't ask my teenager to help out much with the little ones. She tends to have other things on her mind these days and none of those include watching her younger siblings. So anyway, my five year old showed up with one of the Harry Potter books...and a game.

I said to her, "Do you think it's a good idea to get a toy so close to your birthday? Remember, we can here to get a book."

She looked up at me and for the first time I saw a glimpse of the beast that would soon be inhabiting my precious little girl and it looks just like the one who's taken over my first born. She snapped, "It's not a toy, Mom, it's a game. A game is definitely not a toy. I know the difference between a game and a toy."

Remember how I said this wasn't my first day on the job? Well, I wasn't kidding. I didn't want to lose my temper, but I didn't like the way this knucklehead was speaking to me. I simply pointed my finger in the direction of the "non-toys" and said, "Go put it back." She did it, but made sure I could hear every one of her footsteps as she did what she was told. I was beginning to regret my decision to come here and attempt to do something as a family. I don't even like these people part of the time. Why do I want to subject myself to this kind of torture? I should have just gone to Blockbuster, rented them a movie and one for myself and called it a day.

Just as I was beginning to regret my idea for more family togetherness, I turned my attention to my middle child. And she looked happy—even happy to see *me*. Ah, maybe the day would be saved. You can always count on your middle child—that's what I always say...or will start to say from now on. She smiled at me—a really big, toothy grin, and that's when I saw the red flag. I turned my head to the side, trying to read the title of her book. And when I read it I immediately felt heat washing through my entire body, starting with my head and moving down to my toes. *Everything You Ever Wanted to Know about Sex* was the name of the book she was holding. I wanted to vomit, but instead mustered the fakest smile I could, trying not to look fazed, or shocked, or whatever the word is I was looking for.

"This is the book I want you to read to us," she beamed proudly.

I tried to remain calm. I mean I've had the sex talk with my oldest and she was totally grossed out and said she would never do that with a boy or anyone—and then she raked me over the coals, asking me how I could have done something like that—four times! I didn't know what to say to that so I told her that her father made me do it. Was that wrong?

Anyway, my 11 year old and I haven't exactly had "the talk" because I thought I had a few more years before that tragic reality. I guess I was wrong. Is it me or do kids seem to know way more about sex a lot sooner than when we were kids? Now, standing before me with seemingly innocent eyes, was my eleven year old. And I was about to have the sex talk in the middle of freaking Barnes and Noble.

"What do you have there?" I asked as if I didn't know.

She rubbed her hand across the front cover and asked, "What is sex?"

I looked toward the ceiling and began talking to nobody. "Really? This is *really* the way this is going to go?"

"Mommy, who are you talking to?" my daughter asked as she craned her neck upwards, obviously trying to see who I was questioning.

"No one, sweetie," I recovered. "Um, let's talk about this at home, okay? In the mean time, why don't you find another book—maybe something more age appropriate?"

She looked defeated. "But I want *this* book. And I don't want to talk about sex at home; I want to talk about sex right now!"

Her voice was getting louder and a couple of people standing close by turned towards us when she said this last thing.

I smiled at the nosey folks, assuring them that I had everything under control. I bent down closer to make better eye contact with my middle child, who was quickly becoming my least favorite. I said in a calm voice, "sex is an expression of love between two people." I know, I know, lame, but it's all I could come up on such short notice. Oh! And then I thought of something else.

"And, it's also whether you're a boy or a girl. That's your sex."

She turned her nose up at me. "That doesn't even make sense, Mom."

"Well, it's the truth," I said back to her and thinking our conversation was over (or at least I hoped it was) stood up and began making my way to the cashier. She could just get a book another time. I had to get the heck out of here.

As I walked away from her she shouted, "Can I have sex with you? I love you. Can I have sex with my sisters? I love them—and what about Daddy and Granny?"

I turned around, completely horrified. I couldn't get to her soon enough to shut the little devil up. People were staring and whispering to each other and I wanted to die! I grabbed her by the arm and pulled her off to the side. Sweat beads were forming on my forehead and I tried taking a few deep breaths so I wouldn't kill her on the spot. My other two came around the corner and found the two of us. I'm glad my teenager had my 5 year old with her because I'd completely forgotten about her.

"Mom, we've been looking for you," my 13 year old said, obviously annoyed.

"I'm coming—just a minute," I snapped back. I was about to kick some serious butt. When I turned to face her again, I saw it. I saw the look on her face and I knew. She was toying with me. She was doing this to me on purpose and she was obviously enjoying herself. She's turning to the dark side as well. They've gotten to three of my children and it was time for war. And to think, I had birthed these ungrateful children and even waited really late in labor to get my epidural. And this is the thanks I get. Well, we'll see about that.

I composed myself, stood erect, and folded my arms across my chest. I said to her, "You know what? You can have sex with anybody you want to. You can have sex with your brother and your sister, and your granny, and even the dog if you want. Does that answer your question?" Ha! That'll shut the little devil up! I was going to beat her at her own game.

Her face went from cocky to horrified and embarrassed in a matter of ten seconds. I think she even got tears in her eyes. I didn't care. Something was wrong with my children and I momentarily considered finding a book on exorcism, but then I decided it would be better if we just left as fast as we could, before CPS showed up to take them from me—although, that wouldn't be the *worst* thing that happened today.

"Now let's go!" I said a little too loudly. Not one of my children said a word as we made our way out the door, bookless. That was a stupid idea anyway. Spending time with the family—ridiculous!

But on a much happier note, I had prevailed. These little twerps had messed with the wrong girl. And I was going to enjoy the sweet smell of victory, however short and fleeting. The car ride home was quiet. I cranked my eighties music and sang along to Prince, and heard nothing from the back seat—not a peep. Like I said, it's not my first day on the job. Oh, and if you're keeping score at home: Super Mom—1, silly children who try and mess with Super Mom—0.

About the Author

Shauna Glenn lives in Fort Worth, Texas with her husband and four kids—three girls and a boy. She is not great at anything but good at several things, like cooking, sewing and power shopping. She has a vast knowledge of things that a regular person might find completely useless and a waste of time, like any and all things related to celebrities and the birthdays of people she went to school with twenty years ago. Her passion is designer handbags and Mexican food, and her favorite alcohol treat is a tall glass of Pinot Grigio. In her opinion, writing is cheaper than therapy, but she has decided that all proceeds from her book sales will go directly into a "future therapy" fund for her children.

Check out Shauna's website: www.shaunaglenn.com

You can contact Shauna directly at shauna@shaunaglenn.com

Printed in the United States
118323LV00004B/200/P

9 781434 384539